A LITTLE BITE OF MAGIC

LITTLE MAGIC BOOK ONE

M.J. O'SHEA

CHAPTER ONE

The old place was pretty gross.

Frankie didn't want to admit it, but he wasn't blind. It kind of smelled too. Like maybe there was some old milk rotting in a fridge somewhere. But it was his *dream*, his tiny corner of a big city and he refused to give up on it. He'd already worked way too hard and come *way* too far.

He'd gotten out of Vieux Chene, Louisiana, tiny town full of judgmental family members and people who only thought they knew him and he wasn't going back, no matter how dilapidated his new restaurant currently was. Frankie was determined to love the place. Even if it killed him.

"Isn't it great, Dom?" Frankie turned to look at his best friend from culinary school. He didn't need to hear an answer. Didn't mean Dom wasn't ready with one.

"You're nuts, Frank. This place is a rat trap."

Dom had come for moral support.

Some kind of support. Frankie elbowed him in the side.

"No, it's *Cucina Capri*. At least it will be."

Frankie had come up with that name years ago when he was surfing the internet for cooking school applications and dreaming the far-off fantasy of his own restaurant anywhere in the world that wasn't Vieux Chene.

Dom snorted. "More like *Cucina* Shithole."

Dom had a point.

Frankie cringed at the plaster walls that sagged listlessly. They'd degenerated over time into a color something like that of an old, worn-out sock. Not what he'd call appetizing. The floors hadn't fared much better—speckled linoleum, worn away in the corners, and riddled with small, suspicious bite marks. He didn't want to think too hard about the bite marks. Probably meant rats. Frankie hated rats.

A pitted aluminum door at the threshold between the dining area and his future kitchen swung off one rusted hinge. It swayed precariously back and forth in the brisk breeze of the San Francisco spring afternoon. Frankie pushed on the heavy old door gingerly, afraid that it would come off its remaining hinge completely. It would be his luck to have the behemoth fall on his foot. He didn't have the time for injuries, didn't have time for anything that could get in his way.

There was magic to be done.

San Francisco was his place. This restaurant was his place. He could feel it in his bones.

Dom laughed out loud at the sight of the kitchen.

"Is this about what Sofia told you?" Dom asked. "Seriously, man, you don't have to do all this just to get laid. I'll take you to a bar or something. Easy peasy. How long has it been anyway?"

Too long.

Frankie snorted. "None of your damn business. This isn't about what Sofia said."

"Are you sure?"

Sofia, his cousin back home in Louisiana, had premonitions.

More than that, really. When Sofia said something was going to happen, it happened. So when she called him that night a few months ago and told him in a rather embarrassed voice that she saw him in a warm brick-walled kitchen making out with some ripped out guy, legs wrapped around his waist, well Frankie had taken it seriously. But this *wasn't* about Sofia.

It wasn't. At least not totally.

"Don't make my life's work into a pathetic plan to get some action."

Dom raised his eyebrows. "You're the one who told me about it."

"I know." And, boy, did he wish he hadn't. "I just think this is the right place... not because of the brick walls."

But there *were* brick walls. Just like the one his cousin told him about, and cavernous ceilings and big paned windows. Frankie had nearly gasped when the real estate agent had let him in. There was also a huge pot rack that hung, rusted and barely grasping the hook screwed into the ceiling nearly twenty feet above. The floor was flagstone, and the sinks deep enameled cast iron. His ancient beast of a stove and giant brick wood burning bread ovens might have looked like they were from another century, but it was exactly what Frankie wanted— a kitchen built for slow-cooked, homemade taste.

"Oh, Frankie," Dom murmured in a falsetto voice. "Take me now."

He wrapped his arms around himself and made obnoxious smooching noises. Even though Dom was joking, Frankie's spine tingled with momentary warmth. He shook himself out of it.

"Screw you," he said on a laugh. "Leave my restaurant alone. I didn't stomp all over your dream of becoming a corporate food minion."

"Dude, you've got *powers*. You wouldn't have to be a minion. You could be a corporate food *god*."

"Hey! Ix-nay on the owers-pay, right? You know I wasn't supposed to tell you about that."

Frankie shot Dom a quick glare. Damn, he wished he hadn't told. Again. No one was supposed to know, family rules and all that.

"But can't you do all that *woo-woo* shit?" Dom made a wiggling motion with his fingers. "You want me as executive chef. Hire me today," he intoned.

Truth was, it was harder to charm humans than most would think. Pretty stubborn creatures.

Besides, he didn't want to go that route. Most of the time, he pretended his powers didn't exist at all.

Frankie had left Louisiana, and his big overbearing family as soon as he could get the hell out of there and he didn't plan on going home any time soon. Ever if he could help it. Making gorgeous food was the only magic he was interested in.

He punched Dom in the arm again for good measure.

"I told you I'm not doing that stuff any more. I also told you I'm not supposed to talk about it. You *can't* know."

Dom snorted. "I know nothing. Especially if I ever meet anyone from your family. Which seems doubtful after how many years of you hiding me away from them?" He picked up a mangy old wooden spoon and dropped it back onto the butcher block. A puff of dust exploded into the air and practically danced, glimmering in the afternoon sun that streamed in from high casement windows. "Besides. It's not my fault you've got loose lips after a shot or two of Patron. I didn't exactly *ask*."

Frankie sighed at the memory of the very convincing demonstration he'd given Dom of his powers. He'd acted like a flaming moron that night.

It really wasn't his fault, he'd tried to reason to himself. Witches didn't have a high tolerance for regular human alcohol, okay? And as much as he tried to deny it, that's what Frankie was and always would be.

Just like his mother, his cousin Sofia, and the rest of their annoyingly talented extended family.

Frankie was... a witch.

C*HIRP* ....*Chirp...chirp...Chirp...chirp...*SHNEEEPPP

Addison reached over and slammed his hand into his alarm until it stopped making those awful noises that echoed in his head like a missile siren. He didn't need the alarm anyway. He had been awake for close to an hour. Addison knew he probably could've gotten his morning workout in, but he didn't want to get up. He never wanted to get up. Getting up meant going to work, eating more weird food, talking to his boss and Julia and his mo—

The loud ear-splitting squeal of the alarm was replaced by his phone, which he'd forgotten to silence the night before. The opening chords of *Carmina Burana*. Harsh and weirdly perfect.

Mother.

"Hello?" He tried to sound like he'd been asleep. Sometimes she left him alone if he was convincing enough.

"Addie, have you picked out a wedding venue yet?

Because I saw this gorgeous park with a gazebo over by Chinatown and—"

"Mother." Addison's head ached already, and he hadn't even gotten to his ten o'clock mocha slump yet. "First of all, I've been asking you to stop calling me Addie since high school. Second of all, Julia and I are waiting until our finances are more solid."

That was bullshit.

As far as he knew, there was no actual reason, beyond total disinterest, that neither of them had pushed for a date. He didn't really wonder what that meant. He'd meant it when he proposed to Julia. Sort of. They'd been together for so long and his mom and Julia both thought it was time. It *had* been time. But the longer they waited to walk down the aisle, the less Addison seemed to care about it. He wasn't sure if he ever had.

"Love doesn't wait for finances, Addie."

She never listened to him. Especially before he was caffeinated enough to deal with her. He supposed that was part of her job description.

"Mom, I'm thirty-three. I think I know what I should be doing with my own life, thanks."

She huffed and...wait? Was that sniffing? "I hate when you say stuff like that, Addison Albright. It makes me feel useless."

Sigh. It was never a good sign when she resorted to both names. He needed a diversionary tactic. "You know that's not true. Listen, Ma, I need to get ready for work. Can I call you tonight?"

"Are you going to ask your editor to switch you to the sports desk?"

It had worked. Something new to nag him about. "Mom..."

"Okay, okay. I'll talk to you later tonight. But ask Doug about the sports column. It's been so lackluster lately."

"I will." He had no intention of doing anything of the sort.

Addison hung up the phone with another sigh. Two sighs already, and he wasn't even out of bed yet. Not a good sign for the day to come.

It was time for his morning routine—fifty push-ups, a hundred sit-ups, two sets of twenty squats, then twenty-five minutes on his treadmill. He did it every morning. Exactly the same. Addison wasn't much interested in changing his routine. He wasn't much interested in change in general.

After his workout, Addison took his work clothes—folded neatly over the easy chair in the corner of his bedroom the night before—and went for a shower. Exactly fifteen minutes later he'd shaved, showered, and was in the kitchen pouring his breakfast: plain cereal with milk. Toast, light butter, no jam. The same thing every single day, just the way he liked it.

That was Addison Albright's biggest irony.

Addison was the food critic known as The Phantom Foodie. He swooped in, unannounced, to review a new restaurant twice a week. The restaurant only knew he'd struck once his, usually snarky, review surfaced in the paper.

But he was the opposite of a foodie. He liked things plain, simple, and easy. Cereal, white-bread toast, tea – plain black, none of that foofy herbal stuff – crackers with butter, and plain white rice. He ate salad because it was healthy, not because he wanted it. It should come as no surprise that he hated most of the food he was paid to review.

It was a job, though, and he'd taken it. Choices hadn't

been thick on the ground when he was a new graduate with a shiny journalism degree. He'd spent a number of years doing odd jobs before he had gotten his first offer. He grabbed it rather than spending yet another year painting trim and weeding gardens. Even if it wasn't his dream job, he at least was writing.

Off to work. Addison patted his stomach with a groan. The Phantom Foodie was about to strike again.

CHAPTER TWO

SOOOO...PERHAPS THE RESTAURANT RENOVATION business was more involved than Frankie originally envisioned.

It had been nearly three weeks, and they weren't done yet. He'd never admit to Dom that he was in over his head. He'd never admit a damn thing to his parents. The project was just a bit overwhelming, that was all. He had it handled. Frankie refused to be anything but a success.

Luckily, he had a good chunk of the Vallerand money to play with and that it'd come from his grandmother Stella, so his parents didn't have a damn thing to say about it. Quite a lot of it had already been burned through with contractors, supplies, and permits.

He'd gotten the moldering drop ceilings removed first and was glad to have been right. There was a tall, vaulted ceiling above. It had been covered with years of spiderwebs and rat droppings, but with a few well-placed traps and some whispered encouragement—okay, okay, so he used his gifts sometimes—the wildlife moved on and his restaurant was creature free.

After that, and some very extensive cleaning, he painted the walls a soft, warm color somewhere between a haystack and a ripe autumn pumpkin that reminded him of his grandmother Vallerand's chateau in Avignon.

Frankie had done a bit more fudging on his self-imposed rules when he decided he wanted a mural of grapes, flowers, and vines along the west wall. It wasn't his fault he couldn't paint like that, at least not with his hands. The mural looked fantastic, anyway, by the time he finished. The afternoon sun hit it just right. The walls would transport his customers from urban San Francisco to a golden late summer in Tuscany. Perfect.

He'd found some old, scarred maple flooring and mismatched but homey tables and filled the room with fabrics in wine, purple, and green. His last project was the kitchen—his kingdom.

Even though it had looked atrocious at first sight, it had required the least work. The oven functioned perfectly, and the rest of the mess was solved surprisingly easily with some screws and of course more cleaning. His kitchen passed inspection, along with the dining area, and all of the required licenses had been filed and paid for. Right about then Frankie's stomach began to flutter. It was nearly time.

The only thing left to do was plan his first menu. Since he'd been revising it over and over practically since birth... well, that just left panicking. And he had plenty of time to do that.

~

Cucina Capri opened with little fanfare and even fewer customers. Frankie had expected it—hoped for something different, but expected it all the same. His menu was a robust mushroom stew his grandmother used to make filled with herbs and wine, paired with chewy freshly baked rosemary and olive Foccacia. He had a nice selection of wines and vanilla custard with blackberries. He also had a ton of leftovers. The few patrons who'd come in had raved about the fare. Frankie hoped the raves turned into recommendations. His Vallerand money would only last so long.

But over the next few weeks, while Frankie experimented with soups and sandwiches, desserts, pastas, and quiches, his dining room slowly grew more crowded, and the noise of happy customers rang cheerily through the doorway into his kitchen. Frankie was relieved. There was no way he could ever crawl back to his family in failure.

On a rainy Wednesday, close to a month after Frankie had opened his doors, he finally had his first full house. His newly hired waiter, sweet but bumbly Owen, had his hands full running big earthenware bowls of potato soup back and forth from his kitchen to the diners. Frankie had baked loaves of cheddar-topped sourdough to go with it earlier, and the whole place smelled like cheese and bread and home. Exactly like he'd always wanted.

Owen came bustling back into the kitchen with an empty tray. He nearly tripped on a raised section of flagstone but managed to right himself. "Three more soups, two cobblers, and the woman at table eight wants to know how much a loaf of bread is to take home."

"Coming right up!" As Frankie responded, he turned and placed two of the individual peach cobblers on a rack in the brick oven to warm. He tried not to notice that Owen nearly tripped again, on nothing but saved himself from disaster at the last moment. The poor guy was doing far better than when he first started. Truthfully, Frankie had always had a soft spot for strays, and Owen had lost puppy written all over him.

He removed the cobblers from the oven, topped them with a dollop of cinnamon whipped cream, and gave them to Owen, who'd just returned from delivering the soup.

"Tell the woman on ten it's four dollars for a loaf and if she wants I can bag it at the end of her meal so it's still warm when she leaves."

"Yes, sir."

"Frankie," he corrected.

"Um, Frankie."

"Hey, what do you think of eggplant parm tomorrow with a chicken Caesar and chocolate almond mousse?"

"Everything you make is good, sir."

"*Frankie.*"

Owen cleared his throat uncomfortably.

"How old are you, Owen?"

"Twenty-two." Owen did enough lip biting and foot shuffling to make even Frankie nervous.

"Well, I'm twenty-five so I'm way too young to be 'sir' to you. Frankie is perfectly fine."

"Okay." Owen looked at the ground.

"Hey, Owen, you're fine. Just no more 'sir.' And here's another cobbler. Didn't you say table six wanted one to share?"

Owen's face blanched a bit. "Um, no. I was going to, but..."

Oops. "I must have overheard. These walls are so thin."

The walls were brick, and he knew it. Pretty sure Owen knew it as well. His hapless employee took the proffered cobbler and escaped.

～

"Are we going to meet Jim and Lacey at The Golden Orchid tonight?"

Julia sounded hopeful, not necessarily because she wanted to do something with Addison, but because she wanted to parade him around her friends like she always did. He was *exactly* the kind of man she'd planned on marrying someday, or so she said when they'd first met.

"Jules, you know I get tired of eating out. I have to do it so often for work." Even through the phone he could see her eyes widen. He hated that fake angelic look. It made him want to cringe. "Maybe you should have another boyfriend for public appearances."

"Addie, that's not fair—and don't say boyfriend. You're my fiancé."

Has she been hanging out with my mother? "Fine. Is seven okay?"

"Yes, it's great. I'll see you at the restaurant."

He rarely picked Julia up, even more rarely saw the inside of her apartment. She never ever came to his condo. He'd found a unbelievable deal on a gorgeous place with cherry floors and a big bay window, which just happened to be a block off of Castro Street. Neither Julia nor his mother approved of "that neighborhood." He didn't really care one way or another about what went on in his neighborhood. At least his mother and Julia left him alone more often than they would if he lived somewhere else. In his mind, that was one of the top selling points of the property.

"I'll see you at seven at the restaurant." Addison hoped he didn't sound too resigned. He felt resigned.

"Oh, Addie?"

"Addison," he sighed. No more lunch dates with his mother for Julia. They rubbed off on each other too much.

"Yes, of course. Addison. Will you please wear your

navy sports coat tonight? It looks so nice with your eyes—oh, and the sky-blue button-up underneath."

Navy sport jacket, check. Blue shirt, check. On display for perfect Julia's perfect friends...yeah, check that off too. Addison looked in the mirror and ruffled his hair from its neat side part. A tiny rebellion perhaps, but it felt good. He had to admit the blue shirt did look nice with his eyes. Julia was always going on and on about how they looked perfect together—two blue-eyed blonds. Sometimes it seemed like appearances were all he and Julia had in common.

He sat at The Golden Orchid with Julia, who'd annoyingly worn a blue sweater thingy that matched his shirt almost perfectly, and listened to Julia babble with Jim and Lacey, who also matched in that 'couples who end up looking like siblings' kind of way. He didn't pay attention to their conversation. He picked at his dinner, which Julia had ordered for him, and thought of what he'd seen the night before.

In his neighborhood, there'd always been no shortage of, well, *interesting* things to see. He'd watched men kiss, women kiss, sometimes groups of them walking down the street cuddling and holding on to each other. Interesting. But what he'd seen the other night...that was far beyond interesting. He'd gone to sleep dreaming of it and woken up hard as a rock.

There had been nothing different, nothing particularly special about them, just two young men, clearly on a first date. They were perched on the stoop next to his, kissing. It wasn't just the kissing, although that was enthralling in itself; it was the touching, the way the boys didn't even notice him standing there with his eyes superglued to them.

It was the overwhelming feeling that there wasn't another soul in the universe for either of them in that one perfect moment. It hit Addison in the gut hard.

He'd never felt that way about anyone before—certainly not about Julia. There'd never been room in his neat little world for something that all-consuming. As he sat there with his matching girlfriend – no, *fiancée* – who, well to be honest, he didn't want anymore than the Burmese noodles he picked at, Addison wondered if he could handle that kind of passion.

Yes, he decided. *I could handle it.* Even more than that, he wanted it. Addison wanted to feel that intoxicating delicious *want* just one time before he signed up for an easy, but boring, life filled with matching sweaters and dinner parties with the Laceys and the Jims who would fill his world.

All I want is just one perfect kiss.

CHAPTER THREE

"Hey, Albright, I want you to check out this new hole-in-the-wall place over in Cole Valley today. It's been all over the Bay Area's Instagram tags lately."

Addison looked up from the review he'd been in the middle of.

He tried to make his column funny, if typically not very favorable. The sarcastic snark had started because he didn't care for a lot of the overwrought food he had at the trendy eateries around town. It had continued because he'd become controversial, known as the critic who was impossible to please. The readers loved it. His editor loved it. People, apparently, looked forward to laughing behind their hands at whatever successful restaurant The Phantom Foodie had shoved down the verbal drain. He didn't get it, but like he'd said to himself a million times, it was a job.

"But, Doug, I thought I was going to that seafood place down on the Fisherman's Wharf."

Doug dropped an index card on his minuscule desk. "Here. It's an oyster something or other."

"Oysters?" Addison's stomach clenched.

"No. Cucina Capri. They call it an... *osteria*. It's some Italian word. It's one of those places where they only make one meal a day and everyone comes and eats it anyway." His editor snorted. "Lemmings."

"No choices?" He felt the indigestion starting already. Addison opened his desk drawer and pulled out a huge bottle of Tums. Looked like it was going to be one of those days.

The place was right off of Cole Street, and hole in the wall was an apt description — although a rather pleasant hobbit hole it seemed to be. Cucina Capri. It sounded fancy, but if it was described as an *osteria* in its press materials that was a good thing. Addison now knew an *osteria* was more like a pub with family style food. Casual. Maybe it wouldn't be so bad.

Pregnant bursts of steam wafted out into the late spring air from the open front door. Addison read the chalk-drawn menu. Salad with garlic bread. Garlic bread, *ahhh*, yes, that's what he smelled. And pumpkin tortellini in a rosemary-lemon alfredo sauce. Addison inhaled and was pleasantly accosted with herbs, butter and cream, and the salty tang of garlic and parmesan. The smell ended with the mellow sweetness of cooking pumpkin. Odd, but for once he actually wanted to eat it.

"Please choose a seat, sir." A young girl with a curly strawberry-blond bun gestured to the room.

There weren't very many empty seats. He chose one by the window. It was plush and velvety with a lovely view of the shady sidewalk. A rather awkward young man came to fill his drink order and ask which items he'd like from the day's menu. Addison said he'd like both the salad and the pasta and would also like a slice of the lemon raspberry torte they'd listed for dessert.

He always had to order every course. Usually he dreaded it.

Cucina Capri was different. It wasn't pretentious, trying too hard to be hip, wrapped up so tightly in image that the love of food was lost forever. It was, however, a place where he'd like to relax, sit back with a book and a room full of pleasant smells, and just be. Addison hadn't been anywhere like that in a long time.

He took in the aged gold walls, the mismatched but perfectly fitting furniture, the gorgeous mural that transported him to another place and time. He sighed, but instead of his usual resignation, it was...satisfaction? Yes, that was it. Addison hadn't ever been so content to sit in a restaurant and bask in its atmosphere.

The awkward waiter brought him his pasta and a crisp salad along with a thick slab of herbed garlic bread that Addison couldn't wait to sink his teeth into. The top of the pasta bubbled up gooey and cheesy, and the sauce smelled like fresh lemony heaven. The salad was bright green, and the bread, oh, the garlicky goodness. Addison didn't know which to try first—a dilemma he wasn't used to. Everything about it was full of flavors and textures and enveloping smells, things he usually didn't like. But the food was captivating—like that kiss he'd witnessed.

Addison lifted his fork and took his first flavorful bite, and *oh* it was everything it had promised to be. The pasta melted on his tongue, silky and creamy with a rounded citrus bite. The salad was perfectly dressed, the bread chewy, and his dessert, fruity and creamy with a crumbly butter crust, sent chills rushing up and down his spine.

It was heaven. Pure heaven.

Whatever this chef had done must've been some sort of culinary witchcraft. Addison thought his feelings about food might be changed forever. He wanted to try *more*.

"I LOVED IT, DOUG," he announced the next morning. "The food was actually delicious, atmosphere was simple and homey. Here's my write-up."

His editor looked non-plussed. "You never love anywhere. You don't really like food."

"You knew that?" Addison had been trying to hide that weird quirk of his since he'd been hired.

Doug chuckled. "Of course. It makes you the perfect food critic. We seem discerning and restaurants are scrambling to figure out our secret—it's the recipe for greatness."

Addison couldn't help feeling used. "Well, I liked this place." He dropped the document on Doug's desk. In the age of email, his editor still liked to get a hard copy in his hand. He skimmed over the review.

"This doesn't have your usual...flare. Style."

"What do you mean?"

"I mean The Phantom Foodie is no fun if he *likes* the restaurant." Doug's face twisted in thought, his lips pursed.

"But I did like it."

"Yes, yes. But there's something missing. Surely they did something you didn't like."

"You want me to look for problems?"

"Yes!" Doug crowed gleefully. Addison wondered if he'd been hitting the sauce. He usually saved it for the hours with two digits at least. "You're a critic. *Criticize.*"

"And if I don't find anything to criticize?"

Doug leveled him with a sober stare. "Then perhaps we'll find someone who will."

Addison sighed. *A puppet. That's all I am. To my mother, my fiancée, my boss. A goddamned puppet.*

SHEETS OF SOAKING rain sluiced down the restaurant's windows. Frankie looked out into the gloom. His dining room was slow, practically empty. Too bad, really, because he'd outdone himself with the gratin he'd made that day. It burst with layers of potatoes and zucchini coated in parmesan and bread crumbs, paper-thin slices of sweet Italian sausage, and loads of fontina cheese oozing lusciously between the cracks and bubbling all over the top —the perfect comfort food for a chilly, rainy day.

He sat on the counter, eating a giant chunk of his caramel bread pudding and taking a breather for the first time in weeks. Owen came in with his tray. He looked out of sorts, but for Owen that was typical.

"What's up, O?" Frankie tried to keep the kid on his toes.

"Um, there's a situation, and um, me and Bethany don't know what to do."

Bethany was his hostess, less flustered than Owen, but a bit of a lost cause on her own, constantly moping about whatever loser of a boyfriend she'd managed to pick up that week.

Frankie put down his dessert. "What is it?"

"Well, this woman, at table four"—just in case Frankie couldn't tell her from the six other people in the room —"she's been crying and we don't know what to do."

"Did you ask her what was wrong?"

"Bethany said she was talking on the phone to a friend. Her husband just left her." Owen stuck his head out through the doorway. "Oh, her friend just walked in. They're hugging and the woman is—"

"Owen." Frankie had to interrupt the play-by-play before it lasted the rest of the afternoon.

"Yes, sir—Frankie?"

Sir Frankie. Mom would love that.

"Go offer those women a dessert. On the house."

"Y-yes." Owen gave Frankie an owlish look and turned heel for the main room.

Frankie sliced off two squares of his pudding and placed them on plates. He lifted the old, pitted wooden spoon Dom had found the day he'd first bought the place. After he thoroughly sanitized it, the spoon had become his favorite tool. With a smile, he dipped it into the caramel sauce.

He didn't even think about it, just concentrated on a good feeling—fulfillment, hope, maybe a touch of laughter. Those feelings came from his chest and travelled down his arm.

"Better. Everything is better," he whispered, and let the caramel sauce stream off of his wooden spoon until it drizzled over the puddings and onto the two plates.

He thought it might have worked, but no one ever accused him of being a charm expert. He started to laugh at himself for being dumb. All of a sudden, though, Frankie felt an odd electrical sensation on his hand, like his palm was being soldered to the handle of his spoon. It wasn't particularly unpleasant, but it was oddly...permanent. He shook his hand a few times, but the tingling sensation never completely receded.

Just then, Owen came back and said that the two women would love the dessert. Frankie nodded and then shook himself to get rid of the last few strange moments. Owen looked at him with his head tilted.

"Take the desserts, Owen. It's fine. I just got a weird chill."

Owen nodded and then picked up the two puddings and carried them to the dining room. He hopped back up onto his counter with a glass of water and his pudding.

François Vallerand! What have you done?

Frankie jumped and nearly spilled his water

Hello, Mother. If it were possible to feel her huff from across the entire country, he would have.

Frankie knew it irritated the hell out of her when he didn't respond sufficiently to her dramatics.

Jesus, is she always watching me?

Frankie hated the fact that she could jump into his head at will. He wasn't powerful enough to do it back to her... even if he'd wanted to, which he didn't. She could transport physically too, with a bit more effort. Frankie tried his best to avoid any situations that would cause her to do that.

"Do you have any idea what you've done?"

Done? *"I didn't do anything."*

"What are you holding in your hand?"

He looked down. His favorite spoon was still clutched in his tingling fingers. *"A spoon, Mother. Why?"*

Frankie felt a bone-jarring jolt, and then his mother stood glaring daggers at him in the restaurant he'd tried to make Vallerand-free. No such luck.

CHAPTER FOUR

BRIGITTE VALLERAND WAS TALL FOR A WOMAN, AND imposing. She looked Frankie right in the eye, and he was nearly six feet himself. She'd swept off her hair off her face in a high ponytail. Frankie thought the severe hair, black slacks and sleeveless tunic were a bit much even if she was going for witch chic, but he knew it was best to keep his opinions to himself.

"Why are you here?" he asked.

His mother yanked the spoon from his hand and examined it closely before making a disgusted sound. "You've bonded with a spoon." She ground the heel of her hand into her forehead. "A spoon, for Christ's sake! We'll be a laughingstock."

"What are you talking about?"

She smacked him with said spoon on the side of his shoulder. It stung through his shirt at the point of contact. "Would it have killed you to pay attention when you were a boy? Always dreaming of leaving, never learning what you can do."

"Mother. Quit with the lectures. What did I do?"

"No matter how much you wish not to be a witch, you are one. And you've just made this disgusting old wooden *spoon* into your wand, of all things," she spat, and shook the spoon in his face.

Frankie grabbed his spoon from her. He felt protective of it, all of a sudden. That probably meant she was right about what he'd just done. *Shit.*

Just then a wide-eyed Owen came shuffling into the kitchen. "The two women are laughing now, Frankie. What did you do?"

Seemed like everyone wanted to know that. Frankie sighed.

Owen noticed Frankie's mother and jumped back. "Who are you?"

Frankie imagined "and where the hell did you come from" would've come out of Owen's mouth next had he not bitten his tongue.

Frankie sighed. "Owen, this is my mother. She came in...the back door." He gestured to the rusty door next to the oven, the one that looked like it hadn't opened since prohibition.

"Brigitte Vallerand." She stuck her hand out, palm down, ever the aristocrat.

Poor Owen didn't know what to do with it. Frankie made kissing gestures from behind her. He finally got the picture and took her hand, but shook it instead. It was better than nothing.

"Well, I'd better be going, darling."

Darling? I've never been "darling" a day in my life.

Frankie's mother gave him a long look, one that said "you'd better not screw up again," and turned to go. At least she left out the door which she had to pry open instead of vanishing into thin air. Frankie would've had to scrape Owen off the floor otherwise. He was already looking at Frankie like he wanted to drop his tray and take off.

"Um, Frankie? Seriously. What did you put in the bread pudding? Those ladies are laughing like they're at a comedy show. It was like crying one minute and now, boom, instant good times." He sniffed the air. "It's not, you know, party pudding, is it?"

Damn, maybe a bit too much with the mojo. "No, it's not party pudding." He chuckled casually and leaned close, like he was about to share a grave secret. "Sometimes women are kinda nuts," he whispered. "Especially the ones related to me."

Owen smiled uncomfortably and then turned to plate another slice of the pudding without further comment. He went to use Frankie's spoon for the caramel, but Frankie stopped him.

"Here, use this instead." He handed Owen a regular metal ladle.

Frankie didn't want his spoon...*oops*...wand, to fall into the wrong hands. *Jesus.*

Frankie couldn't resist checking on his handiwork, though. The women indeed perched on two plush velvet ottomans he'd found for practically nothing on OfferUp, giggling happily. He wandered over to their table.

"How is everything, ladies?"

"It's wonderful," the crier said. Her eyes were still red-rimmed, but more from tears of laughter than anything else by that point.

Frankie smiled. "I'm Francois Vallerand, the owner.

Please let me, Owen, or Bethany know if you need anything else."

Both women gave him another long look and then burst into giggles. As he walked away, he heard one of them whisper to the other, "We have to bring Cynthia and Nikki to this place. He's gorgeous."

"And that *accent*. I can practically feel the bayou sliding over my skin."

Frankie had to bite his lip to keep from laughing. Yes, definitely a bit too much of the mojo. He'd have to practice.

ADDISON WANTED to quit his job. Right then. He wanted to walk into his pudgy boss's office and slam down the favorable review he'd written about Cucina Capri and tell his boss to take the snark and shove it up his ass. Not that Addison would ever say anything like that without keeling over. He sure liked to think it, though.

The food is simple, yet mouth watering, the atmosphere friendly and homey...

Shit.

The food is boring, simple to the point of mediocrity...

He didn't think he could do it. It seemed so *wrong*.

The atmosphere could be called homey, but felt more like a mismatched set of socks to The Phantom. He wondered if he was at a Victorian rummage sale.

Addison felt like a horrible person, but he managed to go through his review, line by line, and change each sentence of description to match his usual sarcastic style. He hated doing it and hoped no one would read his review. Cucina Capri was *magic*. He'd wanted to go back. He wanted to live in that golden, fragrant room.

Now it seemed like that would be impossible.

"I DON'T LIKE THIS, Doug. It's not right."

Addison's editor rolled his eyes. "What do you care? It's just another flash in the pan. These little restaurants come and go all the time."

"This place is special."

"Are you drunk? You don't say special. Listen, we like ratings. Our readers like snarky Phantom. End of story. You're going to that fish and chips place Monday, okay? The one you were going to hit yesterday."

Addison sighed. "Fine."

He plodded back to his cubicle after that, strangely deflated. His phone lit up with a message from Julia. "Hi, Addie. I know we had plans for movies tonight with Tim and Caroline, but I'm going to have to take a raincheck. I think I'm coming down with a cold. I'll talk to you tomorrow."

No "I love you." No emotion. But also no double date for the evening. Addison's relief filled him, quick and palpable.

"Hey, Albright, a few of us are going to that new wine bar right off of Hartford and 19th. You wanna go?" He looked up. It was Jillian, one of the features writers.

"You know that's in the Castro, right?"

"Is that a problem?" She looked like she was waiting for him to be judgmental.

"No, actually, I only live a few blocks from there." *Live a little, Addie.* "Sure, I'll go. What time?"

"Really? You've never accepted one of my after-work invitations before. Well, anyway we were thinking eight-ish." Jillian smiled, girly and surprised.

Addison nodded. It was nice to make people smile. Perhaps he should do it more often. "I'll be there."

~

FOUR HOURS later Addison stared at the shirts in his closet. What did one wear to a wine bar in the Castro? Huge butterflies beat around his stomach, wings flapping hard. Addison felt ill. It was just a wine bar, damn it. He could do this.

He had been wanting to go out without Julia and her perfect-matched-set couple friends, right? He needed to let go, to see if he could feel something even remotely close to what he'd witnessed that night outside his building.

Addison wasn't going to *do* anything. Not really. It wouldn't be fair to a whole list of people. But it sure was nice to dream, to plan something that wasn't really going to happen. It added a bit of excitement to what even he could admit was a pretty bland life.

If anyone needed a bit of excitement, it was him. He picked a shirt, telling himself not to obsess about it, and jammed that and a jacket on. Then he walked out the front door and locked it before he could talk himself out of it.

The street was colorful and bright with its rainbow flags flapping and neon signs flickering in the dimming twilight. Sidewalks were lined with Friday-night diners, couples holding hands, friends laughing. Addison drank it in with a smile.

He found himself scanning the strolling people for that dream he found himself having when he let himself — deep voice, wide shoul—was he fantasizing about men again? It was a part of him that he tried to squelch as much as possible. A large part.

Julia would be horrified. His mother would have to be hospitalized.

He found the wine bar that Jillian had been talking about. A small group of employees from the paper sat at a corner table, talking and laughing. Jillian waved him over with a smile.

"Hi, Addison."

"Hey, guys." He tried to sound casual, like he wasn't scared out of his wits. He pulled up a chair.

"We've got a merlot here, but if you want something lighter we can call the waiter."

Addison nodded and forced himself to relax. "That would be good, I prefer whites."

Jillian chuckled. "I should've figured as much." She waved at a white-shirted waiter, and Addison smiled, settling into his chair and pretending that he did things like join friends for a drink all the time.

I've got this.

"What is this place?" Frankie squinted at the sign over the door.

"There's wine here, you'll like it, quit asking questions." Dom pushed Frankie through a swinging glass-paned door into the clinking warmth of the bar.

"Mmm, something smells fantastic. Whatever it is, I want it."

"C'mon, let's go sit at the bar."

The bar was dark and romantic, candle-thrown shadows flickering sexily. It was mostly filled with men—there were women, in a group by the corner, a couple clearly on a date, and one hanging on the arm of a guy who was looking Frankie up and down like he might want to lick him.

Frankie wasn't interested. Anyone who looked at him like a juicy hunk of steak wasn't his guy.

He sat at the bar with Dom, who ordered a chardonnay and scanned the room.

"What are you looking for? You're making me nervous." Frankie chuckled softly, but it was true. Dom's behavior had him on edge.

"There's this guy I met at the market last week. He said he comes here Friday nights sometimes."

Frankie snorted. "Oh, now I see. I'm a safety blanket. Thanks, dude."

Dom elbowed Frankie. "I'm looking out for both of us! I thought maybe you could get some action too. I mean, unless Sofia's little premonition came true and you've been holding out on me."

"Shut up." Frankie rolled his eyes.

"That's what I thought. Beaujolais?"

"Sure."

Dom flagged the bartender down and ordered Frankie's glass and a basket of herbed cheese straws. Frankie sipped at the wine and slouched on his stool. He hadn't realized how tired he was until he'd sat still.

It was the first night he'd let himself take a break from the restaurant since it had opened. They usually closed right after dinner, but he stayed late doing accounting, working on recipes. It really never ended. His restaurant had a good first two months, despite the harsh review from *The Chronicle's* critic The Phantom Foodie, which had deflated him for days.

Even though things had gone well so far for the most part, Frankie was bone-deep exhausted. It would've been nice to flirt with a guy, or perhaps even more, but the effort wouldn't be worth the—

"Hi, can I please have another glass of the Chateau Ste. Michelle Pinot Grigio?"

Frankie felt him without even turning around.

Seriously.

Whether it was his hereditary sixth sense or just a strong reaction to that sexy molasses voice, Frankie's entire body burst into waves of pleasure. He inhaled and picked out something woodsy and fresh, with a touch of sandalwood...and saltwater? He saw candles flickering in a beach house and flashes of sleeping in with the window open so salt air could flow in over their naked backs...wait a second. *Their?* What the—?

Frankie had to turn around. He ditched Dom in the middle of a sentence and swiveled in his stool to come face-to-face with the palest set of blue eyes he'd ever seen. The other man looked surprised. Frankie was as well. He hadn't meant to get right in the stranger's face. But that was the odd part—the man didn't *feel* like a stranger. Frankie didn't know him, was pretty sure he'd never even seen him before, but those eyes. They were so...

"Hello," Frankie said. He mentally chastised himself for such a lame opener.

"Um, hi." Blue eyes smiled hesitantly. His awkwardness made Frankie melt.

"What's your name? I'm Frankie." He stuck out his hand. Frankie could've been accused of lots of things, but shyness wasn't one of them. Good thing, because the gorgeous guy who smelled like heaven looked like he had his voice stuck in his throat.

"Addison," he finally choked out. "My name is Addison." Then he reached his hand out to shake Frankie's.

The touch felt like a puzzle piece falling into place. Perfect. He saw the possibility of how good it could be between them all in a flash in that one odd moment—the house he'd never seen, sleepy Sunday mornings in bed kissing, a Dalmatian curled at their feet. *A Dalmatian?* Frankie smiled. He'd always wanted a dog.

He wanted all of it.

CHAPTER FIVE

A DDISON LOOKED AT HIM WITH WIDE EYES. F RANKIE shook out of his momentary cloud. He didn't want to scare this one away.

Frankie cleared his throat. "Addison, huh? That's unique."

He got a wry smile for his efforts. "Sometimes I hate my mother."

Frankie laughed. He couldn't help it. That low voice was sexy and self-deprecating, and he wanted to hear more. "Me too." He gestured at himself. "François."

"Ouch."

They chuckled together. The bartender brought Addison his wine, and Frankie panicked for a moment. *Damn. Come up with something brilliant so he doesn't walk away.* Frankie turned to Dom, but he'd disappeared while Frankie was busy trying to get his pounding heart to calm down.

"Your friend is over there." Addison pointed. "Were you looking for him?"

Frankie followed his gesture. "Oh." He chuckled. "Looks like Dom is busy. Do you want to sit here for a while?" He hoped that sounded casual. Really, Frankie wanted to hog tie the guy to the bar and kiss him breathless.

"Sure." He got another one of those hesitant smiles. "So, um, Frankie, what do you do?"

"I'm a chef."

Addison looked a bit uncomfortable at that. *What's wrong with being a chef?* "Where do you work?"

"You've probably never heard of it. Little place. Cucina Capri. It's in Cole Valley, right by the Haight."

"O-oh. I'll have to check it out." Addison turned pink.

Frankie smiled at his awkwardness. It was adorable. Addison had to be at least twenty-seven or twenty-eight, but he acted like a bumbling teenager. Frankie loved it. Made him feel experienced.

"I think I can arrange that," he replied with a smile. "What do you do?"

"I work at a newspaper."

He was lying about something. Or evading. Frankie could easily tell. His face turned red and he looked at the counter. Why he was lying wasn't so apparent. Maybe he just worked in the mail room or something and was embarrassed by his grunt job. Frankie nodded and let the topic go. He didn't want to do anything to make Addison walk away.

It took Frankie an hour or so, and a few more glasses of Pinot, to get Addison to loosen up. Once he did, they had a great time talking. Frankie wasn't surprised. Addison was flirty and had a sharp, sarcastic sense of humor that Frankie loved.

They talked wine and food and San Francisco versus Louisiana. Addison told him his Southern accent was sexy.

Frankie blushed, which he hadn't done in years. They shared the basket of cheese straws and another of fried zucchini with a creamy pesto dip. In between comments to Addison, Frankie decided he was going to have to experiment with something pesto based soon. He hummed around a mouth full of zucchini. Addison smiled and handed him another.

"Don't you like it?" Frankie asked. He suddenly realized he'd eaten far more than half of the crunchy-soft zucchini slices.

"I think I might be in the mood for dessert," Addison answered with a wink.

Frankie moaned. He wondered if Addison had any idea how dirty he'd just made that sound. *God, he's hot.*

"I think I can arrange that," he said again. "If you really want some."

Addison had been rubbing his free hand absentmindedly along Frankie's jean-clad thigh while they talked. He nodded and stood. "You want to go say good night to your friend?"

Frankie looked over to where Dom had a tan blond laughing at his jokes and leaning closer and closer. "I think he's fine." He did take out his phone to text Dom that he was leaving. "What about your friends?"

"They left a long time ago."

Frankie vaguely remembered Addison's friend Jillian giving him a big grin and a thumbs up as his group had slipped out the door.

"Um, do you want to go to your place?" Frankie asked as soon as they were on the street. He knew how it usually worked. He had a feeling it wasn't the same with this one, though.

Addison hesitated. Frankie wondered it he'd read the

man all wrong. "I do, but my mom has a key and an awkward habit of showing up on Saturday mornings."

Frankie chuckled. "Don't worry. I know all about mothers who pop in unannounced. My place is on Potrero Hill, but I know somewhere closer." He took Addison's hand and laced their fingers together. Addison seemed surprised at first, but then sighed and smiled.

Frankie was nervous, which was strange, since he'd decided he wasn't going to have sex with Addison. He realized as soon as they stood to leave the bar that this one was too important for a one night stand. Maybe that was the source of the nerves, the lack of a clear agenda. Or the fact that he already wanted there to be a future with this guy.

There had been boyfriends before, of course, but he'd never felt a stomach-flip of such magnitude. It was tripping him out. He'd never gotten a picture so clear and immediate before either. He hadn't been as good at reading people since he stopped practicing his magic. Maybe it had come back a little since the spoon incident.

"Here's a cab. I didn't drive." Frankie waved the cab down and gave him the address for the cafe.

The ride was short but filled with tension, the good kind where both people are intensely aware of each other and not quite sure what they want to do about it yet. Frankie didn't let go of Addison's hand. Instead he played with it, tracing his fingers across the back, clasping and unclasping.

He wanted to kiss him—had the whole time in the bar, watching those lips talk and tongue lick up droplets of wine from the rim of his glass. Addison might seem uptight, but the man was a sensual creature waiting to be released. Frankie couldn't wait to see what happened when it finally happened.

"Here we are," he said when the cab pulled up to the curb. He dug the key out of his pocket.

"Are you going to get in trouble for being here?"

Frankie chuckled. "From who?"

"Um, your boss?" Addison looked so unsure. It was adorable.

"I am the boss. This is my place. Come."

Addison froze for a moment, and Frankie laughed again. He held out his hand and tugged Addison into the darkened restaurant. Frankie always left the smaller of the kitchen lights on. He led them through the maze of dining tables to his kingdom.

"Dessert. Hmm. What'll it be?"

IT WAS *HIS* PLACE? Frankie? Addison's stomach twisted. He couldn't believe he'd been flirting all night with the man he'd panned so unfairly in his review. Of all the guys in San Francisco, why him? Addison knew immediately he should tell Frankie what he'd done—who he was. The thought of that gorgeous face falling was enough to make his stomach clench again.

I can't. I shouldn't be here.

That much was obvious. Addison really hadn't planned on doing anything. Really. He was just going to talk to the beautiful man in the wine bar then go home and fantasize about what could've been. What could never have been, actually, since he *wasn't going to do anything.* So why was he there, with said beautiful man, in a deserted restaurant kitchen about to do what was definitely something?

Because I want to. More than anything I've wanted before.

Frankie was dancing around the kitchen, clearly in his element, taking out ingredients and cookware.

"What are you making?"

He grinned, that sweet flashy smile that made Addison's belly weak. *I want to touch him again.* It had been heaven simply holding hands. Who would've thought his routine day would end in such an amazing way? He had expected to have a glass of wine and walk himself home. Alone. Instead he was with a gorgeous chef in an old restaurant kitchen that should've been creepy, but was instead atmospheric and wonderful.

Addison didn't want to wake up from whatever dream he'd landed in. Telling the truth would result in a short ride back to reality.

It's okay. Just for tonight. I don't have to tell him who I am if I never see him again...

Frankie poured cream and cracked eggs into a glass bowl. He made the motions look graceful. Effortless. Even when he whisked it all with a big metal thing that looked like a torture device.

"Are you going to tell me what you're cooking?" Addison couldn't believe he wanted to know so badly. Even though there was nothing really happening yet, he smelled magic on the breeze. Wait, there was a breeze? There was. It was subtle and warm and sweet, but didn't seem to have an origin. "Where's that wind coming from?"

"It's a surprise, nosey, and what wind? The door is closed." Frankie cocked his head to the side and listened. Addison didn't feel anything.

Weird.

Frankie put the bowl of cream and eggs over a pot of water that he set to boil. Then he started splitting black stalks that looked like beans over the bowl and scraping out the tiny bits of seeds until they were swirling in the cream before dropping the pods in whole. The vanilla smell was instant and intense. Frankie added a cascade of sparkling sugar and began to stir with an old wooden spoon.

"I get the vanilla beans from all over. These ones are from Mexico. The flavor is gorgeous. It's sexy and rich."

Addison's mouth watered. He wanted sexy and rich. He wanted to feel it on his tongue. Frankie sprinkled in a spoon of white powder.

"What's that?" Addison asked. He sat on a stool opposite Frankie's cooktop. He couldn't stop staring.

"A bit of cornstarch. It helps everything to get nice and thick."

Why does everything he say sound so damn hot?

Frankie kept stirring. He concentrated hard, eyes closed.

"What are you doing now?" Addison had never seen anything like Frankie cooking.

Frankie grinned at him. "Just adding the magic touch. My relatives are...very French. I got some odd customs from my mother's side of the family."

Addison nodded. *Ahh.* Frankie poured a small measure of liquid into the warming mixture. It was amber-dark and rich and caught the light as it trickled from his measuring cup.

"Rum." Frankie grinned wickedly. "Can you handle it?"

Addison's head swam. The steam coming from the pot was enthralling, stirring his belly and settling in his chest. He felt warm and melty, like he could close his eyes and float. Frankie leaned his head over the bowl and inhaled. Addison wanted to lean closer too, to the bowl and Frankie. He wanted to inhale and kiss and taste and...*ohhh.* How much wine did he have?

"Needs some caramel, I think," Frankie murmured. He took a jar from the ancient monster of a refrigerator, stirring and murmuring until the golden ribbon of gooey sugar was all gone, dissolved into the swirling creamy white.

"Are you talking to the food?"

Frankie smiled. "I think all chefs do. Here, taste." He took another spoon and dipped it into the warm mixture.

Addison leaned across the island before he could think and let the spoon slip into his mouth. The flavors melted across his tongue, filling him until he was tasting and inhaling and reaching out to cup Frankie's jaw in his hand.

"Good?" Frankie's voice was a rough whisper.

"Amazing."

"Here..." Another spoonful found its way into Addison's mouth, even more intoxicating than the first. He savored the exotic flavor, licked the sweet warmth off of the spoon. Frankie moaned.

"What?" Addison asked. He felt even looser than he'd been at the wine bar, although he knew it was impossible from just that small taste of rum. His body was heating up and opening and he wanted to *touch*.

Frankie sucked the rest of the custard from the spoon. "You," he answered. "Do you have any idea how sexy you are?"

"Can I have more?" Addison asked.

They shared another spoonful, then another, then a third. The haze got thicker in Addison's head. Frankie slowly drifted his way around the island, the custard spoon in his hand. He wriggled his way in between Addison's thighs. Then he dipped the spoon again and brought it to Addison's lips.

I need to kiss him.

Addison licked rich rum-scented caramel cream from

the spoon again, savoring his odd high, and leaned forward. Frankie's hips nudged closer. Addison wanted to get closer still.

"Can I...?" Frankie whispered.

Addison nodded. *Yes. Please...*

Their lips touched, just barely at first, and Addison breathed in Frankie's sugar-scented breath. *More.* He had to taste. Addison's fingers found their way behind Frankie's neck; his tongue swiped along a lush lower lip. The taste, oh the taste, it crawled down his spine with sweetly stinging claws of pleasure. Addison shivered.

Then Frankie slipped his tongue out and tasted Addison's lips, just like he'd been tasted. The moment was excruciating and perfect, sweet and a little wild.

"Is this okay?" Frankie asked.

"God, yes," Addison breathed. He barely recognized his own voice.

"Good, cause I need more."

Frankie lifted his arm and threaded a long fingered hand through Addison's hair. He pulled him close until their mouths collided in a kiss so intense Addison wondered if he'd be able to breathe once it was over. Frankie moaned against his mouth, or maybe it was Addison who moaned. It didn't matter.

The result was pleasure. Hotter and sweeter than any he'd ever thought possible.

He tasted dessert and something more that he knew had to be Frankie—warm, rich, and sexy as hell. He heard the distant clang of a spoon on flagstones, but it barely registered. The only thing he was aware of was the swirling, consuming, gorgeous flavor that bloomed between them and the heavy sexual haze that he couldn't surface from. He didn't want to surface anyway. Ever.

Frankie pressed closer. Addison couldn't drag him close enough.

"I want to keep kissing you all night," Frankie murmured, his voice breathless.

"Yes," Addison answered. "All night."

And just like he'd always hoped, the rest of the world disappeared.

CHAPTER SIX

ADDISON MADE IT HOME AND INTO BED JUST AS THE
sun rose blush pink along the horizon, with his mind and his
senses full of Frankie. The mop-topped chef with pale skin
and pretty brown eyes had enchanted him body and soul.
He spent Saturday in bed, staring at the ceiling, unable to
sleep. All he could do was touch his lips and try to capture
just a small morsel of what he'd felt the night before.

He'd never kissed anyone like that in his life—not Julia
or the few people he'd dated in college, not even Mark Sulli-
van, who he had kissed in high school behind the theater
curtains when they'd both been stage crew at the spring
musical senior year. That moment had been the hottest of
his life until Frankie. Until he'd eaten caramel custard and
tasted real romance. That consuming kiss that up until then
he'd only seen from a distance. It was his to cherish.

But it couldn't happen again, no matter how much he
wanted it. That wasn't the life he was meant to live. That
fact was hammered in when his phone rang Saturday
evening. He was lounging, uncharacteristically, on his

couch in a pair of warm-ups and a tank top. The idea of returning to his regularly scheduled life was unbearable.

"Frankie?" he asked excitedly without checking the caller ID. *No, you jerk. Frankie doesn't have your number. He just gave you his.*

"Addison, this is Julia. Who's Frankie?"

"Oh." *Damn it.* "He's a friend from the paper. I mean, I met him when I was with some friends from the paper...I mean he's a friend."

There was a long silence on the other end of the phone. "Are you okay, Addie?"

"Addison. And I'm fine."

"Well, you'll be glad to know that I'm feeling better as well. We don't have to cancel our dinner plans with Karen and Bobby."

Fuck a duck. He'd forgotten about dinner with Karen and Bob. They owned a fancy bed-and-breakfast up on Nob Hill. They also tended to match somehow. Even their hair was pretty much the same color.

"Jules, I'm not sure I'm up for dinner."

"You're not sick, are you? I can call your mother."

Oh, great, because that would make everything just peachy. "No, no. Just tired from work. It was a long week."

"Maybe you're burnt out. You should ask Doug to switch you to the sports section. Or maybe Home and Garden."

"I'm fine, Jules."

If you can call sitting here spinning in my lust and guilt 'fine'.

"Well, good, then you can pick me up in an hour. I'll be waiting outside my building."

"Can't you come get me? I don't feel like driving."

Julia sighed. "You know I don't like your neighborhood. Plus, the gentleman always drives."

Is this really what I'm signing up for?

Addison wanted out. Now more than ever. Just a few perfect kisses and he knew that Julia was wrong for him. Hell, he'd always known but now? It couldn't be more obvious.

But for the moment, until he knew what to say, it was easier to go to dinner with Julia and yet another sweater couple than to argue with her until she called his mother.

Addison dragged himself off the couch.

"What do you want me to wear?" She'd made him go home and change before. He wasn't in the mood.

"Wear the lavender button-up with your black v-neck sweater. It's chilly tonight."

"Can I wear jeans?"

Julia laughed. "Heavens, no. It's dinner, not a hoe-down."

Addison made a face. He'd gotten his jeans at Nord-strom, not the country western store, and they were worth nearly a month's rent in any other city.

"Fine." Addison tried not to sound like he was sighing. "I'll be there in an hour."

HE MANAGED to last until Tuesday before he felt like exploding. Three long days where all he could think about was Frankie's taste, the slick slide of Frankie's tongue in his mouth, the way those slim hips fit so perfectly between his thighs.

I have to go see him.

Calling was out. Addison knew he'd just get tongue-tied

and awkward and end up hanging up without saying what he wanted to say—which was that he needed to see Frankie again before he went insane. Like literally batshit insane. It was possible to go nuts from needing to touch someone and not getting to, right? Addison felt like he was close to insanity whether it was possible or not.

"Hey, Albright. A few of us are going out to lunch. Are you game?" Jillian, his coworker and new friend, leaned on his desk. She smiled at him and gestured over to where a group was congregating by the door. A few of them smiled and gestured for him to join them. He would, but...

"I'd love to, Jillian. I have plans, though."

She nudged him with a grin. "You mean with the hottie from the wine bar?"

That's exactly who he meant. He nodded and tried to conceal his grin, but it mustn't have worked because Jillian squealed and gave a thumbs up to one of his female coworkers waiting near the door. They exchanged air high fives.

Addison was embarrassed but happy that he made the choice he'd been dying to make since Saturday morning. He wanted to see Frankie again. Strike that. He needed to see Frankie again. So he left work early and walked to Cucina Capri, site of the best night of his life bar none.

～

THEY WERE KISSING, hot deep kisses that tasted like vanilla, caramel, island rum, and sex. Frankie's tongue twined around Addison's, his fingers buried deep in soft sandy hair and *oh, the taste*. He couldn't get enough. Addison's knees gripped his hips unconsciously, and Frankie's insides melted at the thought of those legs hugging his hips bare, opening for him, taking him in...

"Frankie?...Frank?...Hey, space-o!"

"Oui...?" Frankie looked up. "Oh, hey, Dom. What's up?"

"Dude, you okay?"

Frankie smiled. He was okay. Sort of. Screw that. He was going insane. It had been three days, and they'd kissed and kissed for hours, and it was sexy and gorgeous and perfect and *argh*! Why hadn't Addison called?

Frankie wanted to see him again. He'd wanted to drag him home and spend the whole night kissing and then some. It had been so hard to tear himself away as they'd kissed goodbye on Addison's doorstep at dawn. He'd wanted *more*.

Sure, they'd both gone a bit out or control in the kitchen the other night. He'd hit that *dulce de leche* hard with the happy sauce. It had been impossible to resist. But far after the spell had to have worn off, they'd kept kissing and touching and getting as close to each other as they could. It wasn't just the custard anymore by the end of the night. Frankie knew. He could tell the difference. It was *real*.

"Hey, I asked you a question."

"Oh, yeah. I'm good."

"I'll say." Dom thrust his hips crudely a few times in Frankie's direction.

"*Pshhh*. It wasn't like that." Frankie couldn't help smiling. What it *had* been was so damn perfect...

"And why not? You bitch out?"

"No. We kissed."

Dom made a face. "You just kissed? You're lame."

"We just kissed for hours. And it wasn't lame. It was

amazing." His breath caught when he remembered just how amazing it had been.

"And where's lover boy now?"

"At work."

I think. I wish I knew.

Frankie had thought the other night was the start of something. His charm was just supposed to nudge Addison past his shyness, not to make him feel something he didn't really feel. So what if he was out there somewhere going about his everyday life like the other night had never happened? What if he barely remembered it had happened at all?

That would suck so bad. *Impossible.*

He *had* to feel it for real. There's no way that one little spell had been an all-nighter. Half the time the effects of his little charms didn't last more than a few minutes, sometimes even just a fleeting moment.

"Hey, I was going to walk over to grab a latte at Cosmo's. You want one?"

"Hmm? Oh yeah, please. I'm zonked." Not really, but he needed a few minutes by himself and Cosmo's was sure to have a long line this time of day.

Frankie wanted to talk to someone who could give him answers, but that was really only Sofia. He was a little worried about calling his cousin. She was just... so much better at that stuff than he was. She wasn't an asshole about it like his mother was, but part of him hated to admit how behind he was.

He was going to lose it if he didn't have some answers, though. Or at least a bit of reassurance that it wasn't a one time thing that she saw.

Frankie pulled his cell out of his back pocket and called. He wasn't good at jumping into people's heads like his mom was. Plus, it was rude. Sofia picked up after a few rings.

"Today must be absent Vallerand day." She chuckled.

"What?"

"Just talked to Arlo a few minutes ago. He's in Seattle and I told him he should come hang out with you for a while."

Sofia's younger brother. Frankie had always liked Arlo, never got why he seemed to prefer being a bit of a vagabond instead of settling down but he supposed they all had their quirks.

"Arlo is always welcome, of course."

"What's up? You sound all stiff like auntie Brigitte."

"Suck it," he told her. Sofia chuckled. "I guess I'm just having a bit of a problem."

"Yes?" She drew the yes out impatiently with sass only Sofia could manage to put into one word.

"You remember that vision you had? Of me and the guy kissing in the kitchen?"

"I'd rather not, but unfortunately yes," she said dryly. "A bit too much info for the blood relatives."

"Do you remember what he was wearing?"

"Plaid shirt I think. Khakis."

It was a different night. Frankie's belly fluttered hard. That meant that either it wasn't Addison and he was all wrong or Addison would be back. He seriously hoped it was the second one.

"You think you could come take a look at my kitchen?"

Sofia grinned. "Sure. You alone?"

"Yeah. For a few minutes at least."

"Text me an address and a picture of the place. That always helps."

Sofia hung up and Frankie texted her the address and a shot he'd taken of the outside right when he first opened. He only had to wait a minute or so before Sofia was standing in his kitchen, a bit out of breath but grinning.

"That was a rush. I haven't gone that far before. Good thing I had a small lunch."

Frankie rolled his eyes. "Your mom's going to kill me."

"It's fine." She giggled then looked around. Her eyes grew wide. "So I'm guessing you want to know if this is the place."

"Y-yeah. Is it?"

She cleared her throat and blushed. "Definitely the place. Definitely."

"Good to know."

"Does that mean you've met him?"

Frankie shook his head at her wicked grin. Maybe it was a mistake to call his far too wise cousin.

"So, what's on the menu today? Smells awesome."

Frankie was stirring with his spoon...*er*...wand. He'd done nothing more than infuse the broth with a faint feeling of well-being. Nothing that anyone would notice. He just liked making people happy.

Sofia had gone, just in time for Dom to return with lattes and a doughnut for each of them. Frankie had demolished both before he went back to his preparations. His phone had buzzed with a message from Sofia saying she was safely home and she wanted details the next time he saw Addison.

"French onion, of course. Will you shred some gruyere for me?"

Frankie gestured at the block of cheese. Dom worked in

silence for a while, and Frankie sliced small pieces of baguette to put on top of the soup with melted cheese. His broth was a mixture of sherry, beef stock, fragrant herbs, and olive oil. He was waiting to put the onions in that he had sautéing in butter until it was nearly lunch time. He didn't want them to disintegrate in the liquid.

Dom made quick work. He transferred the grated cheese into a plastic tub near where the bowls were assembled. Frankie missed working with him. He hadn't realized how much easier things were when they worked together.

"What's for dessert?" Figured. Dom had a huge sweet tooth.

"There are eclairs cooling on the racks over there. I made a custard to fill them with. Would you mind piping it in? The bowl is chilling on the top shelf of the fridge."

"Yeah, no problem."

"The tips and piping bags are in the third drawer from the bottom," Frankie called before he went back to seasoning his sautéing onions.

Dom worked quietly; his usual sarcastic quips were always quieted when he was cooking. Frankie left him alone. After a few minutes of filling, Dom reached out and wiggled the dial on the radio. A Latin station came on, and Dom turned the radio up. The room filled with the mellow guitar of *bossa nova*. Dom swayed with the beat, dancing as he worked on the pastries.

"This custard is really great, Franks."

"Hey!" Frankie laughed. "You're not supposed to taste. And what's with the music of your homeland over there? You never listen to this stuff."

Dom shrugged. "I like it sometimes when it's rainy. Grandma used to listen to this stuff and say it reminded her of São Paulo, though. I guess it just makes me happy."

Frankie rolled his eyes and laughed. "Whatever. Quit reminiscing and fill those eclairs. I open in fifteen minutes."

"Thanks for helping today, my bestest friend in the whole world, Dom. I know you're tired and this is your day off," Dom said mockingly.

Frankie laughed. "Sorry, dude. I am grateful. We've been so busy lately."

Dom simply nodded and went back to work, dancing the entire time.

It was crowded in the dining room. Owen had his hands full, and Bethany had stopped seating and was running back and forth to and from the kitchen herself, getting bowls of cheesy French onion soup and crunchy cranberry-walnut side salads. Even Dom pitched in, plating and waiting tables after telling Frankie he was going to owe him a case of Stella Artois for his work.

Frankie looked over at one point to thank Dom again for working as frenetically as he had himself. It was then that he noticed Dom was drizzling heated caramel cream onto the eclairs as he plated them. Bethany came and grabbed the plate he'd just finished before whisking it out to the dining room.

Frankie wondered for a second when on earth Dom had had a chance to make a caramel cream sauce, and then he got a good long smell...and encountered bourbon and vanilla and what he knew was a whole lot of trouble.

"Dom?"

Dom licked the cream off of his spoon before he dropped it in the wash bin. "This stuff is amazing. What did you do to it?"

Frankie started to hyperventilate. "Where did you get that sauce?"

"I heated the caramel custard from the top shelf of the fridge. Why, did you need it for something else?"

"I thought you were going to *fill* them with the *vanilla* custard."

"I did, but putting this on top just." He made a kissing noise against his fingers. "It's perfect."

Perfectly disastrous. Oh God, oh God, oh God...

Frankie didn't know what had made him keep the charmed *custard*. Maybe he wanted to relive that night. Maybe he wanted the possibility of it happening again. But if Dom had just sauced a restaurant's worth of desserts with it, Frankie was screwed.

Dom looked over at him. His face was all sweet and melty, just like the caramel sauce he had licked off of his index finger.

"You know," he said, tipping his head to the side. "You have really nice lips, Franks. I never noticed before."

I'm screwed.

He was afraid to look, but he had to see what he'd done ...well, what Dom had done, but it was his own kiss-distracted brain that had caused it, that and the fact that he couldn't stand to throw away the dessert he'd made for Addison. *Shit.*

Frankie tiptoed gingerly to the doorway of his dining room. He was afraid to see what was happening out there. He stuck his head around the corner slowly...slowly ... and...*oh hell.*

It was like Valentine's Day on crack. There were house-wives with strollers holding hands over their tables, single diners staring off into space dreamily, a business man fiddling with his colleague's tie and leaning closer for a tender kiss. Owen was offering a morsel of a filched eclair to Bethany, who was all of a sudden looking at him, not with her usual annoyance, but with big blue puppy-dog eyes. Total. Disaster.

And then Addison walked in.

"WHAT'S GOING ON IN HERE?" Addison glanced around the intoxicated room in horror.

"Oh, it's a date lunch. I hold them every so often." Frankie reached for Addison's hand. "Come back to the kitchen."

He pulled Addison back to the kitchen, where he deposited him on the same stool from Friday night before he rushed back out to the dining area. Frankie's behavior was a little odd but Addison was so happy to see him, he let it pass.

Addison saw a rack of pastries cooling over in the corner and a pot of caramel sauce bubbling away on the stove top. Addison couldn't help leaning over and smelling the caramel. It was like that amazing stuff from the other night. Addison glanced at the door and decided no one would ever know if he had a few.

He piled three pastries on his plate and covered them with a generous ladle of that utterly sinful sauce. He was happily munching away when Frankie came back into the kitchen. Addison wasn't sure what had happened to him in the past few days, but he did know he'd choose the caramel pastry deliciousness over plain vanilla ice cream, his previous dessert of choice, any day.

Frankie looked more relaxed when he returned to the kitchen with his friend Dom in tow. His lips were, if anything, even prettier than they'd been the other night.

Addison wanted to kiss him again. Frankie's somewhat relaxed look disappeared when he saw Addison eating the pastries. He blanched.

"I'll pay for it, I promise," Addison said. "I just didn't have breakfast and I was really hungry."

Frankie smiled then, a bit forced, but still a smile. "I'm not going to make you pay for them, silly." Something flipped in Addison's stomach at the tease. "We cleared out the lunch date crowd and closed early."

"Why?" Addison took another bite of the pastry. He really wasn't *that* hungry, but he couldn't stop eating. Frankie saddled up closer.

"Maybe I just wanted to spend some more time with you." Addison was pretty sure it was an evasion, but Frankie's proximity and his scent mixed with that sexy spicy caramel rum smell was driving Addison wild. He leaned over and kissed Frankie, lips parted. Frankie moaned.

Addison had planned to tell him about Julia. That he was stuck in a relationship he didn't want and he'd break it off with her as soon as he could even if he and Frankie went nowhere. He wanted to tell Frankie that meeting him, eating his food, *kissing* him had changed everything. And worst of all, he had to confess about being The Phantom.

He knew he had to say all of that if they had a chance in hell. But instead all he could think about was how much he wanted to kiss Frankie. And so he did exactly that—he kissed. And kissed, and kissed, until an embarrassed knocking broke them apart.

"Um, the dish guy just showed up," Dom said. "Do you want me to send him in?"

Frankie blushed. It was adorable. "Yeah, I don't have

much for him today but he can get an hour or so on his timecard."

"And what are you going to do?" Dom asked him.

Addison looked at Frankie. "I don't know. What are we going to do?"

Frankie gave him this gorgeous grin. "You're hungry, right?"

"Always."

CHAPTER SEVEN

"You want me to come inside when I pick you up?" Addison asked.

"Yeah. We can say hello and get the stuff I packed for the movie." Frankie didn't know why Addison sounded surprised. They were going on a date after all. Their first real official date. It should be at least a little special.

The past two weeks they'd hung out six times, meeting at the restaurant, or at the wine bar, or once outside Addison's newspaper building. Always informal, never prearranged.

It seemed like, although they never made formal plans to see each other, they still couldn't last more than a few hours without a text or a phone call, and those texts and calls usually turned into them making dinner at the restaurant after it closed, or going to a movie, or once an amazing night of kissing and walking in the park.

"Oh, well, yeah I'll park and come in," Addison continued. "Of course. I just didn't expect—"

"You need my address?" Frankie rattled it off and told Addison he'd see him in an hour or so.

Frankie nervously packed a bag with blankets and wine and was about to go hop in the shower when his living room shook with a telltale jolt.

Oh, shi—

"Hello, François."

"Mother. What are you doing here?"

Another jolt shook the room, this one stronger. A tall, sandy-haired man stood next to Frankie's couch, glancing around distastefully—Frankie's brother, Jean.

"Jean? What is this, guys, some sort of intervention?"

"Nice greeting for your family. *Lord*, how can you live in this place? It's awful." Jean's voice grated on Frankie. His perfect existence grated on Frankie. He didn't have time for their nagging. Not when Addison was coming to pick him up in less than an hour. "We know what you're doing, little brother. It's an embarrassment."

Frankie rolled his eyes. "Why does anyone care what I'm doing? I'm just the family fuck-up. At least I came way out here so you guys could ignore me. It's not my fault that you choose not to."

Frankie's mother glared at the scattered bills and papers on his dining room table. They obediently slid into a neat pile, which she moved into the basket that was sitting on an old hutch he'd found in a flea market.

"You know just as well as I do that you're not out here alone," she said. "Your uncle Albie lives with his partner in La Jolla, and there is a strong coven in Orange County."

"The OC coven? I thought you said they were charlatans."

"They're new money, some even work"—she made a face—"but they have ties to the council." His mother huffed, and Jean nearly growled. Frankie assumed the conversation wasn't going as planned.

"That's not the point. The point, little brother, is that you need to quit this charade and come home."

"Charade? I'm happy here. I like to cook. I like—"

"The newspaper worker?" Jean chuckled derisively. "He's so boring."

"How's Clarissa?" Frankie asked pointedly. She was Jean's wife. Their marriage had been arranged by the high council to tie the Vallerands to her family, the Bertrands. Everyone conveniently ignored the fact that she and Jean didn't much like each other.

"She's fine. Expecting again."

"What is that? Four?" Frankie chuckled. He did miss his brother's two older daughters. He'd never met the younger one. It was a constant irritation to Jean that he couldn't seem to produce a male baby. "Maybe this one will be a boy."

"It's not. Her name will be Francine."

"Keeping up the family traditions?"

"One of us has to."

Frankie shrugged. Jean could do whatever he wanted to. Everyone made their own choices. "Listen, are you two here just to bug the shit out of me, or is there something specific? I have somewhere to be."

"Frankie, language. We don't speak like that."

"*We* don't exist here, Mother. Only I do. Now if you two don't mind..."

His mother sighed. "I wish the old discipline practices hadn't been banned."

"You wouldn't." Frankie rolled his eyes.

"Your father would. Jean, deal with this. I have a dinner to host." His mother raised her eyebrows, and with a considerable amount more noise than necessary, she disappeared.

"Isn't Mom a little too old to be having tantrums?"

"Aren't you a little too old to be acting like your family is of no consequence?" Jean lifted the picnic blanket and the wine bottle from the basket. "You're really...dating this commoner?"

"Oh for Christ's sake, Jean. Mother, I understand, but surely you know better than to buy into all that coven bullshit. He's a journalist. He's smart, makes a good living."

"Listen." His brother looked uncomfortable. "Mother is having a dinner tonight, and she'd like it if you came."

Frankie regarded his brother silently for a few moments. "What does she really want?"

Jean winced. "Laurent is going to be there. She wants to set you up with him."

If Frankie only had a dollar for every time his mother tried to interest him in that snobby ass.

It was never going to happen.

"Laurent again? What's her deal with him?"

Jean shrugged. "He's a strong witch, he has fey blood, his family is powerful. Do they need another reason to want you with him?"

"But he's your—"

"He's not my anything," Jean spat out. "Now are you going to do what your family needs you to do and come to this dinner?"

"I don't belong there, JL. I never did."

"Don't call me that. And yes you do belong. You're a Vallerand."

"I'm a chef, and it's time for you to be on your way." Frankie raised his hand to push his brother out of the way.

Jean snorted. "What are you going to do? Hex me with your cooking spoon?"

He disappeared on a laugh. Frankie sighed. He

wouldn't curse anyone with his family. Including himself. Too bad he didn't have much of a choice in that matter.

FRANKIE WAS in a better mood by the time Addison rang the doorbell. He opened it, smiling. A half an hour before, he'd been ready to ask for a raincheck so he could go to his restaurant and bang pots and pans around until he came up with some great new dish. That was the only thing that usually worked when his family got to him. Not anymore. Addison was the best medicine he could ask for.

"Hey, Addie, you have no idea how glad I am that you're here," he said when he answered the door. *Damn.* Addison looked really hot in his short-sleeved plaid shirt and those low-slung jeans. Not nearly so uptight.

"Why did you call me Addie?"

'Cause that's what you call yourself in your head...oh, shit. Frankie hadn't realized what he'd called Addison until it was too late. He couldn't read minds, exactly. He'd never practiced enough. But strong impressions were pretty easy to decipher, and Addison definitely thought of himself as Addie when he was the most relaxed.

"Um, I thought that's what you wanted me to call you. You said 'this is Addie' in your last voicemail to me." He hadn't, but Frankie was hoping he wouldn't remember that.

"I did? I'd had a glass of wine, but I would've thought I'd remember..." Addison looked baffled.

"Let's just go. I've got our basket packed." Frankie was so caught up in covering his gaffe that he tripped on a corner of the area rug he had underneath his coffee table.

"You okay?"

"Yeah. I was just really tired earlier. Guess I'm still a little groggy."

THE RIDE to the park was quiet but comfortable. Frankie rolled down his windows to let in the soft summer evening breeze.

"You don't want me to turn on the AC?" Addison asked.

Frankie shuddered. Canned air felt awful against his skin. He almost always had a window cracked in his place for fresh air. "No, I don't like air conditioning. I'd rather have the outside air."

Addison nodded. "Me too, actually, but my—well, let's just say most people I've had in my car don't like to be mussed."

Frankie poked him. "They don't like to be mussed? Who've you been hanging out with? Your friends sound lame."

"Well, one of them is my mother."

Oops. Frankie cringed.

"Hey, that's okay. She is pretty lame." Addison sighed.

"You guys don't get along?"

"We get along when I'm doing exactly what she wants me to do."

"Why do I have the feeling that this isn't one of those things?"

"That obvious?"

"Does she even know you're..."

"Gay? No." Addison's eyes went a bit wide, like he hadn't meant to say that.

Addison clearly had issues with the whole thing. Not enough to keep him from kissing Frankie at every possible opportunity, but issues all the same. Probably because of the charming mother he mentioned as little as possible.

"It's okay, you know. She doesn't have to like it. Only matters if you're happy." Frankie reached over to put his hand on Addison's thigh. He was surprised when Addison covered his hand and laced their fingers together. He seemed so uncharacteristically relaxed.

"I have been happy lately." He pulled Frankie's hand up to kiss his palm.

Frankie couldn't help the way his stomach melted. The sunset streamed through the window on a soft waft of air—orange and gold shaded with twilight purple. It bathed Addison's face and hair, turning his fairness into fiery gold. His eyes were black rimmed and beautiful when he turned to smile at Frankie shyly, like he wasn't sure that what he'd done was okay.

"I've been happy, too," Frankie told him.

"You know, I don't usually like to be called Addie anymore. It's what I went by when I was a kid..."

"But?"

"But from you, I like it. Doesn't feel awkward."

"Awkward how?"

"My mom calls me that sometimes, but it was my dad who started it. He was different from her. He would've liked you."

"You think?"

Addison chuckled. "Well, sure. You can cook."

Parking was hard to find at the park—classic movie night was popular in the summer—but they managed to squeeze into a slot not too far from the screen. Addison found a great spot on a hill where they could still see if they lay back.

They both busily started to set up, spreading out the big quilt Frankie had brought and tossing down cushions.

Everything was ready by the time the movie started. That night they were showing *Pillow Talk*. It was dated and silly, but Frankie loved it. Getting to watch it in the park with the fresh air and slightly damp grass squishing underneath his feet was even better. The best part was Addison, strong chest behind him, legs encompassing Frankie's torso, and those arms all warm and snuggly around him. Rock Hudson was in the middle of trying to pull the moves on Doris Day when Frankie reached over to the picnic basket.

"Want some wine?"

Addison tugged him back and nuzzled into his hair. Frankie shivered. That was so, so very nice.

"In a second," Addison murmured, and tightened his arms.

"I brought cheese and crackers too." It was better than saying what he was thinking: *I know what we could be. Never let me go.*

Frankie was pretty sure that would scare Addison. Hell, it would scare him if he hadn't seen it so clearly: the house, the beach, sun and salty fresh air coming in through their window, a blue-and-white quilt covering them as they laughed and kissed and talked. The vision hadn't changed. He still saw pieces of it every time they touched, every time he closed his eyes.

"Cheese and crackers? A chef brought cheese and crackers?"

"And grapes." Frankie grinned and tipped his head back to brush a kiss across Addison's lips. "I guess I'm fired."

"Yeah. Fired." He kissed back and rubbed Frankie's belly through his shirt. "You're..." he whispered, but then he seemed to forget what he was saying in the warmth of the kiss.

"I'm what?" Frankie wanted to know, but he couldn't help kissing again. This time it wasn't wine or charmed dessert. It wasn't anything but him, Addison, and how sweet it was between them.

"You're perfect," Addison whispered. Then he seemed to realize what he'd said aloud and cleared his throat. "Maybe I should have some of that wine."

Frankie smiled. "Maybe we both should."

Frankie crawled over the the basket to grab the bottle. The wine was fey and incredibly strong. Frankie had diluted it nearly by half with mineral water. Undiluted, it would make an average human go insane.

Even witches couldn't drink fairy wine at full strength although they handled it better than vodka or tequila. Watered down, it still did more than regular wine did to loosen inhibitions. Frankie thought he should probably warn Addison, but something told him to keep his mouth shut. How would he explain it anyway?

"This is delicious," Addison said after his first long sip. It was that. Fey wine was both sweet and dry, and somehow it always tasted a bit wild.

"It's my favorite."

They sat in companionable silence, watching the movie and drinking the wine, shoulders touching and fingers brushing against each other's. Addison lolled to the side, leaning more heavily against Frankie. Frankie inhaled, loving his warmth and the way he smelled. He hadn't poured himself much of the wine. Clearly he should've poured less for Addison as well, although it was cute how tipsy he'd gotten.

"I might need to have some of those crackers you

packed," Addison whispered. "I think this wine's going to my head."

"That's okay, isn't it?" Frankie gave Addison a deliberately sly grin. Addison chuckled but reached for the rosemary crackers that Frankie had packed.

"I probably don't need the wine anyway. You do a thorough enough job of going to my head all by yourself."

"I love the things you say to me." Frankie was utterly charmed. Who needed a spell anyway? They kissed, and Frankie tasted the strong, sweet fairy wine, rosemary, and a faint hint of what he knew had to be pure magic.

Addison moaned into their kiss. "What are you doing to me?" he muttered against Frankie's lips.

"*Shhh*. Just kiss me."

Addison seemed to have no problem complying. The kisses began again, wine flavored and deep. Frankie's hands snuck up under the hem of Addison's shirt, and Addison scooted closer and closer on the blanket.

They were lying down by that point, surrounded by people but completely lost in their own hazy world. Frankie wasn't drunk off the wine, nowhere close to it, but he'd lost his mind somewhere in those first few kisses, and he didn't much care to get it back. He wrapped his arms around Addison's neck and burrowed into his neck.

How do I convince this man that I've known for only two weeks that we're perfect together?

It was clear to him—how they fit, how their bodies reacted so strongly to each other's presence. Frankie wanted...well, what he wanted could never happen in a public park. It didn't stop him from thinking it as he slipped his hands underneath Addison's shirt again. They didn't pull apart until Frankie heard a high-pitched muffled twittering from the next blanket over.

He pulled away from Addison and saw a group of girls watching them intensely. He was surprisingly embarrassed. Maybe the fairy wine got to him more than he thought. Maybe it was just Addison. Frankie had never lost himself in a kiss in public like that before.

"You guys are adorable," one of the girls whispered with a big grin. Frankie smiled back. He hoped Addison wasn't too taken aback by the girl's comment. Turned out he didn't need to worry. His...boyfriend? date?...was lying on the quilt, eyes to the stars, tracing patterns with his index finger along the sky.

Oh, wow. Frankie chuckled. Maybe he should've diluted the wine a bit more.

"Hey, Addie, you want to pack it up and head home?"

"Is the movie over?" He ran his fingers through already touch-tousled hair.

"No, but you look a bit toasted. I'll drive your car."

"Okay." Addison looked like he was about ready to agree to anything.

"But you're going to have to tell me how to get to your place, okay?"

"'Kay."

Frankie chuckled and stood to help Addison up. They folded up their blanket quickly and gathered all of the pillows and food into the basket before weaving their way through the crowd toward Addison's car.

"Listen, Frankie. I've got to tell you something."

Addison's stomach jumped, but he knew it was the right thing to do to tell him about the column. Frankie would find out eventually, and Addison didn't want him to get hurt by finding out from someone else. He wouldn't bring up Julia at all. Julia was going to end the next moment Addison had to himself. It had been over for a long time anyway; he'd just been too chicken to do anything about it. Next chance he had he'd call her and she'd be out of his life.

"What?" Frankie's lips were swollen and wet from their kisses and the wine they'd shared at the park. And after. They had been lying on his bed for nearly an hour, still fully clothed, just kissing and talking.

The buzz from Frankie's strong wine had worn off, but he still didn't regret asking Frankie to come inside. He never invited Julia inside, or he wouldn't if she'd ever deigned to come near his place. There was something different about how it was with Frankie. Addison didn't know what was going on, but he knew that nothing was as good as being near him.

Frankie propped himself up on Addison's chest and regarded him seriously. "Are you going to tell me whatever it is you said you had to tell me?"

Addison sighed. He was awful at conflict. "When I said I worked at the newspaper, I didn't tell you the whole story."

"What is the whole story?"

Addison froze. *I can't do it.*

"Listen, I know I assumed you were a reporter, but if you're not it's okay, Addie. It's just a job."

Oh, no. He thinks I'm embarrassed because I have some entry-level job. Addison felt even worse.

Frankie looked at him, sympathetic. "You can tell me another time what it is. I'm really sleepy from the wine. Can we close our eyes for a few minutes?"

Addison nodded. *I don't deserve this man. I'm an asshole.* He wasn't about to get rid of Frankie, though. No matter what, Frankie was his. His. He kissed the back of Frankie's neck and then pulled his comforter over them and cuddled him up close.

"Hey," Frankie murmured, about an hour later. "It's getting kind of late. Do you want to take me home before we're both too tired?"

Addison kissed Frankie's forehead and ran his hands up under that soft t-shirt he'd been rubbing all night. Then he said something that he hadn't expected to say, something he'd never said to Julia and only once or twice to anyone else before her.

"Why don't you just...stay."

CHAPTER EIGHT

Frankie chopped basil happily, humming and watching his huge pot of boiling noodles. He already had fragrant piles of rosemary, grated parmesan, minced garlic, and toasted pine nuts ready to be ground together for a classic bright-green pesto. He planned to mix the pasta together with his fresh pesto, mornay sauce stuffed with tons of mascarpone and fontina cheeses, and a bit of good feeling before sprinkling it with breadcrumbs and olive oil and popping it into the oven to bake. He was going to grill some lightly seasoned red bell peppers, onion, and asparagus to go with it for crunch and freshness.

He didn't have to look up to know that Addison had come in. They'd only seen each other a few times in the two weeks since their date in the park—work had been crazy for both of them lately—but they'd talked on the phone nearly every night until it wasn't even night any longer. He sighed happily when Addison hugged him from behind. It was impossible not to close his eyes and inhale.

"Hey," Frankie murmured.

"Hey." Addison kissed him on the neck. "You smell so good."

"Like garlic?" Frankie chuckled.

"Like you."

Frankie turned for a small kiss, which turned into a bigger kiss, which ended with him on the counter, legs around Addison's waist as they tried to inhale each other. It was a while before they drew back, kissing lightly and hugging close.

"I've missed kissing you." Frankie nuzzled Addison's neck. Four days had been far too long.

"Missed kissing you too. Do I get to see you tonight?"

"Yeah. I got all my accounting done for the week. After I close, I'm all yours."

Addison chuckled. "Yeah?"

"Yeah." His breath caught in his throat.

They hadn't had sex yet, but he wanted to. *Damn.* And their kisses had gotten hotter and more full of touching and petting every time they'd been together since that night in the park.

"What's for lunch?" Addison looked over Frankie's shoulder.

"Pesto macaroni and cheese. They've been requesting it." Frankie made the pesto mac dish more than anything else on his rotating menu, but it was so popular he was cleaned out every time.

"And dessert?"

"Shortbread with a raspberry-peach dipping sauce."

"Mmm, yeah, that's what I'm smelling."

The shortbread was already cooling, flaky and buttery-sweet, on his wire rack tower, and he had the glaze bubbling away on the stove top. He'd added piles of fresh raspberries and juicy peaches to his big sauce pot and heated them up with sugar and a bit of amaretto to add a nice rounded kick.

Frankie slid off the counter to stir his sauce, mashing the fruit and sugar with his old wooden spoon and then adding butter until the whole thing was rich and glossy. Addison came up behind him and kissed his neck again. Frankie hadn't been expecting it, and it tickled. He giggled and jumped. A tingle went down his arm, through the spoon, into the sauce he was stirring.

You've got to be kidding me.

He nearly tossed the whole pot and started over, but then he decided it couldn't hurt. *At least the people will be happy.* He hadn't charmed the pasta dish at least, beyond the usual faint hint of good feeling. At least that was a good thing. Didn't want people passing by to think he was running a comedy show.

Frankie squirmed happily in Addison's arms. "Hey, I gotta get lunch made. I had a line out the door for the pesto mac last time."

"Can I help? I have an hour before I've gotta be at the dentist."

Frankie made a face. "Yuk. The dentist?"

Addison nodded. "But I'll pick you up at your place around eight."

"So you wanna pour the pasta into those big baking dishes? Try to make it even."

"I think I can handle that."

Addison picked up the container of sauce coated pasta, doling it out between the baking dishes. Frankie went behind him and added the breadcrumbs and a sprinkle of oil. It was only a matter of minutes before the macaroni was baking happily in the huge old oven.

"I want to try a cookie." Addison reached out and snagged a piece of shortbread from the rack.

"The sauce isn't ready yet," Frankie lied. It would be a disaster for Addison to have the giggles while some poor dentist was trying to clean his teeth.

"That's too bad. It looks fantastic."

"Yeah?"

Addison nodded. "I like your food. It's delicious but not too foofy, you know?"

"I try to avoid foofy." Frankie chuckled. "I'll save you some sauce for later tonight."

Addison smiled, sly and sexy.

"What?"

"Nothing. You just said sauce and...oh, never mind. I'm a pervert."

Frankie laughed outright at that. "I like it."

"ADDIE, we're going to the theater with Bessie and Charles this weekend. Please make sure your tuxedo has been to the cleaners and is pressed."

Addison sighed. He hadn't wanted to answer the phone when Julia called. Only the fact that he still needed to end it with her made him answer at all. *I should have called her earlier.* She'd been too busy too call him and he was actively avoiding her because he was a chicken. No more chicken for him.

"Julia, there's actually something I need to talk to you about."

Her impatient sigh echoed through his phone. "What is it? I have a pedi appointment in fifteen minutes."

Addison rolled his eyes. Because she couldn't talk to him while some woman painted her toenails…

"I don't think this is working for me anymore, Julia. We want different things." Well, actually they wanted the same thing. A boyfriend.

"Make it work, Addie. We're not breaking up because you're having some mid-life crisis."

"I'm *thirty-three*. And I just broke up with you. It wasn't a question."

"No, you didn't. You said you didn't 'think' this was working for you anymore. I told you it was. Are we done here?"

He knew she was pushy. He knew she typically got what she wanted. Apparently, he'd underestimated just how far he'd have to go.

"Julia, I'm gay. Okay? I'm gay."

He could almost hear her shrug. "That's fine. Now I have to go, I need to go to my appointment and you know I don't like to talk on the phone while I drive."

The call went dead.

"But, Jules, *I'm falling in love with him*," he whispered into the room.

Addison didn't care if she refused to accept it. It was over. He was with Frankie.

ADDISON BUSTLED AROUND HIS TOWNHOUSE, turning on lamps and lighting candles. He was nervous to have Frankie over. Maybe because so much more was implied with this visit than on the last one—that had been all about sleeping and talking. Addison doubted there would be too much of either going on later. At least not the sleeping part.

Their kisses, hell, their dates had gotten steamier and

steamier. The one a few days before had ended with a kiss that had lasted the better part of an hour. He'd had to drag himself away from Frankie before he molested him on the front porch of his restaurant. Also a new feeling.

He tried to put his weird, unsatisfactory breakup out of his head and concentrate on something good, or rather someone good. Frankie. Addison was headed to pick him up in just twenty minutes. He didn't want Frankie to drive over, didn't want him to leave. He wanted to have Frankie in his bed all night and there wake up with him in the morning.

Addison didn't have to work the next day. He could spend it in the wonderfully scented kitchen at the restaurant, helping Frankie cook, kissing, tasting the soft skin of his neck while he stirred some fragrant sauce with his old cooking spoon.

The restaurant had become an extension of Frankie, like part of how Addison saw him. Frankie wasn't Frankie without his cooking spoon or the kitchen at Cucina Capri.

Addison didn't have anything like that to define himself. He wanted to. The Phantom Foodie wasn't him. Not really. It still made his gut ache when he thought of telling Frankie about that. *I should've done it a long time ago.* He figured his hesitation would somehow come back to bite him in the ass.

Addison's phone rang. Shit. Julia. He'd already told her that he wasn't going to the damn theater with her. He had no idea she would be so persistent.

"Julia, what do you need?"

"Aren't you ready?" Impatient as always, her voice rang cultured but still strident through his handset.

"I'm getting ready. For a date. I told you I wasn't going to the theater. I told you we were over."

"And I told you that I bought the tickets ages ago. This date you have can be postponed."

Addison cringed. "Jules, do you not care at all that I'm with someone else?"

He didn't get it at all. She wasn't interested in him, in their relationship, just in making sure she didn't have an empty seat next to her when her friends walked by.

"I care if you're with someone else tonight. We had plans."

He wanted to throw his phone. He would've, if he wasn't worried about it breaking when Frankie might try to call him. "No, *I* have plans. With my boyfriend. I'm done with this conversation."

He hung up on her for once. It felt really damn good. It was time to go get Frankie. In more than one way.

THE SECOND FRANKIE was in his arms, the phone got turned off. It didn't matter. The only person he wanted to talk to had cuddled up to his chest and kissed him hello, no demands, no icy disdain. Just affection— the way it was supposed to be. Frankie had a paper grocery store bag, filled with what Addison hoped was dinner, and a big smile. Addison's pulse jumped.

"Hey, how was the dentist?"

"Would I be really cheesy if I said I needed someone to make my mouth feel better?"

Frankie chuckled. "Yeah. But I'd go for it anyway."

And he did, with another long hello kiss that not only made Addison's mouth feel better, but made his entire body shiver as well.

"You're so gorgeous," Addison murmured when they

broke apart. He was still cupping Frankie's face in his hands. Frankie let out a snorting little laugh and pushed his hand away playfully. "What? I can't give you a compliment. It's true."

"C'mon, Romeo. Let's get in the car." He tempered his cynical remark with a sweet hand threaded through Addison's as they walked down the street to where Addison had parked his car.

"What's in the bag?" Addison asked when they'd pulled away from the curb.

Frankie rolled his eyes and scooted closer. "Lots of drugs."

"That's what I thought. I hope they're good ones."

Frankie snickered. "You seem different. What happened?"

I'm free.

Addison shrugged. "Just had a good day, I guess."

"You went to the dentist."

"I got to see you twice."

Frankie shoved at him jokingly. "No cheese-ball lines."

"Isn't it only a line if I'm trying to pick you up? You're clearly already in my car. Maybe that means it's just the truth."

Frankie's big liquidy-brown eyes melted. "My day is better when I get to see you too," he said quietly.

Addison waited until he pulled up in front of his condo before he leaned over to give Frankie another deep, long kiss. "Let's go inside."

THEY ATE a small dinner of sandwiches and the flaky short-bread with raspberry sauce that he'd been waiting for all day. Addison laughed at Frankie's antics, harder than he remembered laughing before, and felt wonderfully good. It was always like that when he was with Frankie. He didn't have to worry that Frankie was going to disapprove of his clothes — probably, just like Addison, he'd rather they be gone anyway. There was no pressure to fit in with some social crowd he didn't like. There was just laughter and kisses and, well, *happiness*.

They'd taken the cookies to his bedroom, and for once he didn't give a damn if crumbs got on his bedspread. The dipping sauce was so good he wanted to take his fingers and lick out the inside of the Tupperware container. He couldn't stop grinning, even after the cookies were all eaten and his head was in Frankie's lap. Frankie brushed his bangs off of his forehead.

"I don't want to go to home tonight," he said quietly. He leaned over and kissed Addison on the lips.

"No. Don't go home. Stay." Addison snuck his hand under Frankie's shirt and then started pushing it up. It was hard from his angle, but Frankie got the idea. He pulled the shirt the rest of the way over his head and off.

"Your turn," he whispered.

"Yeah."

He'd forgotten how good it felt to have his bare skin against another man's—or perhaps it had never felt so good as it did with Frankie. Addison shivered and touched his back, cupped his hands around Frankie's ass, and tugged him closer. There was no such thing as close enough.

"More skin," Frankie muttered. "I want more."

"*Yes.*" Addison couldn't wait to feel all of Frankie. Every inch of his perfect silky body. He'd only gotten hints before of what it could be like. It was time. They pulled at each other's belts and pants, briefs and socks, until it was all gone and they were wound around each other naked and kissing.

It was perfect.

Addison worked his comforter out from beneath them and cocooned him and Frankie in warmth and darkness. Frankie was beautiful, and Addison loved to look, but feeling in the dark, lips colliding slowly, fingers tracing limbs and muscles and straining flesh—it was intoxicating.

"Addie," Frankie whispered when Addison gripped his cock in his hand and tugged insistently. Addison's breath caught in his throat when Frankie did the same thing. He nearly shouted aloud when Frankie's mouth replaced his hand.

"That's so good," he murmured. "Feels so good."

"Touch me," Frankie ordered when he crawled his way back up Addison's body. "I want to feel you inside of me."

Addison did moan out loud at that. Then he scrambled for the drawer by his bed. Hand slick, he reached for Frankie, for the tender skin behind his balls, the tight opening where all good things could happen. Frankie pushed against his fingers and ground a hard cock against his thigh.

"Oh, God." Frankie shivered and bit down on Addison's neck. "You feel so—" His words were cut off by a loud groan when Addison sank two slick fingers all the way inside.

Goosebumps erupted under Addison's free hand, which was resting on Frankie's arm. It had been a long time, but Addison knew exactly what to look for. And he knew when he found it. Frankie cried out and pressed up against him in a full-body embrace, hands clasping Addison's head and bringing him close for a long, lusty kiss that finally broke when neither of them could last a second more without breathing. Addison kept teasing him, rubbing and touching, letting him grind up against him but not hard enough to come. Frankie panting in his ear was nearly enough to send Addison over the edge.

"Want you, Addie." Frankie's voice was frantic. Breathy. Hot as hell.

"Now?" He smiled.

"Mm hm. Now. Inside. I'm gonna come and I've been waiting *forever*."

Addison understood. It felt like he'd been waiting forever too. Maybe it was the wine they'd drunk with their sandwiches, the same from the park weeks before. Maybe it was just time. He dealt with condoms and lube with lust-drunk fingers. His mouth went dry when he saw Frankie prepare himself.

"C'mere." Frankie pushed him down and crawled over. He seemed to understand that Addison didn't want to be in charge, not this first time. He needed to lie back and bask in Frankie's movement, drown in the grunts and shivers and lusty whispers. And it felt so good. *So good.* Hot and tight and amazingly beautiful.

"Slow," Addison warned. He needed to slow down before it was too late. Too much.

Frankie stopped and grinned breathlessly. He leaned over and kissed Addison slowly, slower than he moved his hips, tongue slipping in all silky and perfectly wet.

"I love..." Addison choked on an inhale when Frankie tightened his muscles and rolled his hips. "*Ohhh.*"

"You feel so good in me." Another kiss, a bite on his shoulder, that wicked tongue tasting the shell of his ear.

Addison shuddered and dragged the pads of his fingers down Frankie's back. "Yes. So good," he repeated.

So good, so good...

Frankie's back was damp with sweat, his face was glowing, and he smiled all soft and sweet before he bit his lip and moaned. Addison couldn't stop looking. He was beautiful.

"Touch me, Addie. I'm going to come."

"Yes," Addison moaned, and tugged at Frankie's cock, hot and hard and wet at the tip. Frankie's foreskin slipped back and forth over steel. It felt perfect. He threw his head back and rode Addison. It was slow and languid but more intense than anything Addison had ever experienced. Deep. Enthralling. Like time stood still.

"Oh fuck, Addie. Now."

Addison squeezed and the warmth of Frankie's release pulsed through his hand and onto his abdomen. Frankie cried out, and his inner muscles clenched down hard. Addison lost it in that moment with a choked scream and a full-body shudder. Frankie collapsed onto Addison's chest, breathless and limp.

"Jesus," Addison whispered as he came down from his high.

Frankie chuckled tiredly. "I know."

They separated momentarily but came back together after only seconds, damp sweaty skin sticking in the most delicious way.

"That was amazing, babe," Frankie whispered.

Babe. Addison liked it. The word felt official. He rubbed the pad of his thumb across Frankie's cheekbone. "This feels good too, just lying here with you."

"It does. We might have to get up and take a shower in a minute. If we don't we'll wake up stuck together."

Addison smiled. "I can think of worse things. Can't you?"

"Yeah." His answer was paired with a squeeze and a kiss to Addison's damp chest. "Don't wanna move."

"Me neither. We'll shower in a little bit, okay?"

"Yeah. A little bit."

~

FRANKIE WAS in the middle of stirring up a vinaigrette for his spinach salad with strawberries and almonds. Addison sat across from him on a stool, painstakingly slicing strawberries to go in the salad. Frankie couldn't stop grinning. *Last night...twice this morning. God.*

They couldn't stop touching each other, even when they'd gotten to the restaurant and allegedly started working. Allegedly. For a long time, work was mainly the two of them kissing and laughing. Even after he really *really* had to start making some food before his customers showed up to an empty restaurant, there still wasn't a minute that didn't go by without a touch, a kiss, Addison tasting the sensitive skin behind his ear...

God, that drives me insane.

Frankie realized he'd have to be careful what he let Addison do while he had his spoon in his hand or his customers would end up having sex with each other on the floor of his restaurant.

Frankie dreamily put down his bowl of salad dressing and floated over to pull the big casserole dish of spinach and chicken enchiladas out of the oven—with his bare hand.

"*Shit.*"

He dropped the glass dish. Yet before it could hit the stone floor and splatter into a huge mess, Frankie reached out and froze it, suspending it in the air. The second he did, he realized that wasn't the best choice he could have made.

Addison stared open mouthed and wide eyed. "Frankie? What the hell?"

Oh, hell.

CHAPTER NINE

"Do I even want to know?" Addison asked warily. He looked pissed. Frankie supposed he would be too if he was a regular guy and his new boyfriend managed to freeze-frame a fifteen-pound dish of enchiladas in mid-air.

"I guess the real question is, now that you just saw that, is it possible for you not to know?"

"True. So then, what? What *are* you?"

Yikes. No hostility there.

Frankie paused for a long time. He didn't want to say it and watch the accusatory look on Addison's face get worse. "I'm a witch."

A lot of reactions would've seemed likely: derision, disdain, laughter. Anger wasn't what Frankie expected.

"Do you think I'm stupid?" Addison's pretty blue eyes were narrowed to slits.

"Do you think I'm lying?" Frankie countered. "You aren't blind. I know you saw what I just did."

"It was a trick. It had to be a trick." Addison ground his nails into his palms. His knuckles turned white. "There's no such thing as witches."

"Clearly there are." *Damn. I have to do it.* "Here. Just hold on for a sec."

Mother, can you come here?

Frankie wasn't as good at communicating as the rest of his family. Perhaps it would've been good to pay more attention in his lessons when he was a kid instead of planning future dishes.

There was a long pause. He thought it might not have worked

Only moments later, Frankie felt the telltale jolt, and his mother was standing in the restaurant kitchen, wearing yoga pants and a big scowl.

Addison shouted and jumped back.

"I was in the middle of Pilates, François. I hope this is an emergency."

"It's not, but you pop in all the time when it's inconvenient. Today, I needed you to do it when it was convenient for me for once. Addison saw something. He needs to know I'm not making it up."

"Well, here I am," she huffed.

"Yes. Addison, my mother, Brigitte Vallerand. Mom, this is Addison."

The eye roll she gave Addison was worthy of every teenaged girl Frankie had ever seen. *Very mature, Mother.* "Yes, he's the food critic who panned your restaurant because he doesn't have the stones to stand up to his boss."

"Mom!" *Wait a second.* "What?"

She shrugged. "It's true."

Addison covered his face with his hands. Frankie stared at him. He didn't know what to process first. Addison was a food critic? The food critic who pann—Addison was *The Phantom?* It didn't make any sense.

"Oh, for Christ's sake, you didn't know?" She rolled his

eyes. "Don't be stupid. Frankie. You do know Laurent is still single, love, if you're done with this..." She made a hand gesture and a disdainful face.

"Mother. Laurent is a pretentious ass. I will never be interested in him."

"He's a highborn witch with fey blood. You could do far worse." She gestured at Addison. "Case in point."

"Okay, demonstration over. Thank you, Mother, you can go back to your Pilates."

There was a distinct popping noise, and then his mother was gone, leaving only the faintest hint of Chanel and condescension.

"I can't believe *you* wrote that article."

"I can't believe you didn't tell me what...*species* you are."

"You lied to me."

"You lied to me too!"

"That's different," Frankie said heatedly.

"How is it different? We both chose not to tell each other something major about ourselves."

"Yeah, but I didn't choose to be a witch."

"Well, I didn't choose to write that article about your restaurant either."

Frankie was about to yell back when he realized what Addison had said. He paused. "Wait...Then why did you?"

"Does it matter?" Addison looked at him warily.

"*Yes* it matters," Frankie sputtered.

"Then I wrote it because I'd have been fired if I didn't. I loved it here that day when I came. I still love it here. Listen, I have the original article if you want to see what I really meant to say. I had to change the whole thing."

Frankie couldn't believe what he was hearing. "So your *editor* makes you be a big dickhead?"

Addison flinched. "No, usually that's all me. In your case, though, yeah, he did."

"Why do you do it?" Frankie couldn't imagine a life spent spewing sarcasm and bad feeling.

Addison shrugged tiredly. "It was a real writing career. There aren't very many out there. I'd been doing odd jobs, painting, lawn mowing. I wanted to be a writer."

"But that's not being a writer, it's being an asshole who spreads meanness."

Addison sighed. "I'll guess I'll just go. Can you get a ride home from someone?"

Addison turned to leave, and Frankie's stomach cramped. *Shit.* "Don't go."

"You're still going to talk to me?"

Frankie sighed. "I'd be a big hypocrite if I didn't. Listen, I don't like what you do but—"

"It's not me. It's just a job, not who I am." Addison looked hopeful. Frankie wished that hope wouldn't end up breaking his heart.

"I guess that's what I was going for."

"So you can be a, well, whatever you are, and I can be a food critic and everything is okay for the moment. Maybe?"

"Addison, I'm a witch. You're going to have to believe that if we have any future."

"We have a future?" Addison made a distressed face.

"I think so, but I'm serious about this. I stopped a dish in mid-air. My mother's a total pain in the ass but she *apparated* right in front of you. She was in Louisiana. She came here. She's back there now in the middle of her Pilates lesson like she was before. I'm a witch. Not a 'whatever you are.' A *witch*."

Addison stood there, staring at the floor, as if the old

worn stones had some sort of answer. "You're a witch," he muttered.

"Then do you believe me?"

Addison sighed. "I guess I don't have much of a choice. Were you ever going to tell me?"

Frankie raised his eyes, and Addison flinched. "Point taken."

"I would have told you eventually. If we got serious enough."

"Last night wasn't serious enough for you?"

"I meant like forever-after serious. I'm not supposed to tell anybody. Ever. That's the only exception." Frankie slouched against his giant old butcher-block and ground the heels of his hands into his temples.

"I don't know about you, but I don't want to be with anyone else. It might not be 'forever-after serious' yet for you, but that's where this was going for me." Addison's voice was small and hurt, but the expression on his face made Frankie's belly melt.

"It is for me too, Addie. It just hasn't been very long. That doesn't mean I wouldn't like us to last."

"See? And now I know your secret so you can't get rid of me." Addison smiled. It was hesitant, but it was there.

"I don't want to. Hey, Addie, um, while we're confessing there's a bit more." Frankie couldn't help but wince. Addison wasn't going to like the rest of it at all.

Addison huffed out a tired laugh. "Lay it on me. I owe you lots of retribution for that review."

"Yeah, you do. So, um, I'll just say it. I charm the food sometimes."

Addison gasped, clearly horrified.

"No no no. Nothing harmful ever. I just put good feel-

ings in it, happiness, laughter...well that one was an accident." Frankie smiled. "You tickled me."

"Wait, what do you mean? You're going to have to spell
this out slowly."

Frankie picked up his spoon. "This is my wand. I didn't
mean for it to happen. I'm a bit of a failure as a witch. One
day a customer was crying and I wished that she could be
happy. My wish went through this spoon and into her food.
The spoon and I bonded and now it's my wand and when I
want people to feel good I can use it to charm their food."

"And have I ever been charmed?"

Frankie could feel his face heating. He winced again.
"Um, yeah."

"When?"

"Well, when you eat the main restaurant dishes, they
usually have a light touch of happiness, and that dipping
sauce, the one I was stirring when you tickled me, my
laughter transferred itself into that...and the first night."

"What about the first night?"

"I might have made that custard feel a bit sexy."

"Might have?"

"Okay. I did."

"Are you saying I kissed you because of some pudding?"
Addison looked ready to pop.

Shit. Not going well. Frankie thought of something.
"Did you want to kiss me at the bar when we first met?"

"Yes. Definitely."

"And do you want to kiss me right now?"

"Not at this exact moment, but in general, yes."

"Then you didn't kiss me because of the custard. You
kissed me because you wanted to. That custard just added a
bit of extra feeling. And I was just as affected that night as
you were, you know. I'm not immune to my own charms."

Addison guffawed. "You might want to rephrase that one."

Frankie snorted, relieved. If Addison could joke, he wasn't that angry. "You know what I mean. We wanted each other. The custard just made it...nice."

"So what have you done to these enchiladas?" Addison smiled slyly. Frankie could see practical jokes blooming in his eyes.

He shook his head. "Nothing. Just baked them."

"What can we do?"

"Addison..."

Addison rolled his eyes. "With great power comes great responsibility, I know."

"I'm not Spider Man." Frankie leveled him with a look. "I just don't want to mess with people. Make them happy, yes. Make fools of them, no."

"And the love fest that was going on that day when I walked in here to find you? Don't give me that date lunch BS."

"No, that was an accident."

"I've heard that word an awful lot."

"It *happens* an awful lot. I told you, I'm not a very accomplished witch." Frankie sighed. "I couldn't bring myself to toss the custard we'd eaten the night you were here. It was sitting in my fridge right near the custard I'd made to fill those eclairs. Dom thought it tasted good so he heated it up and drizzled it on the eclairs. I didn't mean for it to happen."

"Does Dom know about you?"

"He does, but Owen and Bethany don't. My servers can't find out, okay?"

"Why?" Addison shrugged.

"Because *no one's* supposed to know. No one. Dom

doesn't get that either."

"How come he gets to know?"

"Um." Frankie blushed. "It was an accident?"

Addison burst into laughter and reached out for Frankie's hand. He pulled him into a tight hug.

"Are you still mad at me?"

"No, I guess not. I got the food critic secret, and you get this. Just tell me before you charm me again. I don't mind it, as long as it's just for fun. I just want to know."

"Deal."

Addison looked at Frankie's spoon. "So what happens if I touch it?"

Frankie picked the spoon up. He was so ridiculously protective of the thing. "Nothing. Just don't, okay?"

Addison smiled, that familiar comfortable smile he'd only seen pass between other couples. "Okay. Hey, Frankie?"

"Yeah?"

"Are we alright?" He looked hopeful, but unsure.

"Yeah." Frankie smiled. "We are."

CHAPTER TEN

The night was warm and humid, Addison's favorite kind of weather. The sky had filled with dark clouds a few hours before, but the air felt soft, gentle almost. Not even a tiny bite. Perfect. If it rained, that would be even better. He rolled down his window and stuck his hand out to catch the breeze.

"I love that you like to do that," Frankie murmured.

"Why?"

"It's another witch thing." He sounded almost apologetic.

Addison found that since he knew, he didn't mind hearing about it at all; quite the opposite, in fact. He was fascinated with the unique things Frankie could do.

"What about it?"

"We're not very good with enclosed spaces. Always have to have a window open. Barefoot on natural earth of some sort is the best."

"I wouldn't think that would matter."

Frankie shrugged. "I forget why. I guess it's because we're an old species. Have to stay near the earth."

"Is that why you were so happy at the movie in the park?" Frankie blushed again. Addison could see it in the rapidly darkening evening. "Spit it out. Is there more?"

"Well, mostly I was happy because I was with you, and yeah because I was near the earth too. But the wine we drank? It wasn't charmed, but it wasn't human wine either. It packs more of a punch, you could say."

"If humans didn't make it, then who did?"

Frankie laughed softly and shook his head. He said something that Addison couldn't hear.

"What did you say?"

"I said fairies made it. It was fairy wine."

Addison burst out laughing. "Of course it was. Did trolls make the crackers we had with it?"

Frankie snorted. "Everybody knows there's no such thing as trolls." He rolled his eyes as if to say *puhlease*.

Addison reached over for Frankie's hand. As always, he couldn't stand not touching him for very long. He liked that it had nothing to do with a charm and everything to do with real magic.

"You still haven't told me what else you can do."

Frankie shrugged. "That's 'cause I'm not sure what else I can do. I never practiced much. I always just wanted to cook."

"Well, what do you *know* you can do?"

"Charm things, clearly. I'm pretty good at affecting peoples' emotions. That's actually not as elementary as it sounds. People are complex. I can move things, you know, telekinesis, but usually only when I'm feeling a strong emotion like panic. I can talk to my family in my head."

"Can you do that transporting thing?" Addison thought that was pretty cool. Certainly more useful than making sexy pudding anyway. Not as much fun, but useful.

Frankie sighed. "No. That takes a lot of practice. I never managed to get more than a few feet."

"Can you transfigure things?"

He got a huge eye roll. "Do I look like Harry Potter?"

Addison chuckled and poked at Frankie's side. "I don't know. You might be kinda cute with glasses."

"Oh, shut up." Frankie laughed though and laid his head on Addison's shoulder. "Are we almost home?"

They'd been to Addison's house every night for the past two weeks. His belly melted a little when Frankie called it 'home'. "You know as well as I do how far away we are."

"Yeah, but I thought it would be fun to ask." Frankie grinned impudently. Then he leaned over and bit Addison's neck, just for good measure, Addison assumed.

WHEN FRANKIE WOKE in the middle of the night, it was raining, pouring hard and fast and bouncing off the window pane. The air shook with thunder and warm gusts of wet air spilled in the open window—a real summer storm, rare on the West Coast. Frankie smelled it, all wet and green tinged with that odd scent of energy, like the earth was growing. It was when Frankie was his strongest.

"Addie." He pushed against Addison's sleeping form.

Addison rolled over and flopped his arm across Frankie's waist. "It's night still, babe. Go back to sleep."

"You want to see something I can do?"

"Right now?" Addison's eyes opened, but stayed sleepy like he wasn't sure he was really awake. He was so hot when he first woke up rumpled from sleep and sex and still groggy. It didn't hurt that every time Frankie looked at him he remembered all the dirty things Addison whispered in his ear when they were making love.

"Yeah, right now." Frankie couldn't resist kissing Addison's chest. "I can only do it in the rain, and it's probably best if no one's watching, yeah?"

"What exactly does this spell involve?" Addison's eyebrow raised.

"Nothing like that." He bit down lightly.

Addison groaned. "Okay, okay. Getting up."

Frankie enjoyed the white flash of Addison's ass as he rolled out of bed to pull his pants on. He looked back over his shoulder. "This was your idea. You better be getting up if you expect me to."

"I was just admiring the view."

Addison snorted and pulled his sweats back off for a moment to moon Frankie. Then he raised his eyebrows once again. "Well c'mon. I want to see this demonstration. What are you doing?"

Frankie smiled. "You'll see." It had been one of his favorite things to do when he was a kid, something he thought every witch could easily do. It had been years before anyone saw him do it. That's when he realized it wasn't a common talent. Even his mother had been impressed.

After they dressed and shoved their feet into shoes, he led Addison to a small park, which was luckily only a couple of blocks from his condo. Addison shivered theatrically, but Frankie just laughed.

"It's like seventy degrees out. You're not cold."

"It's all wet," he whined. Addison whining might have been the cutest thing Frankie had ever seen.

"Uh huh. Weenie."

"Hurry."

Frankie held out his arms. "Come stand close to me."

Addison moved right next to him. He poked Frankie in the side. "Can you do this without your spoon?"

Frankie had been concentrating, but he opened his eyes long enough to see Addison's teasing grin. "You know what? Just be quiet. No mocking the witch."

"Sorry, babe."

"You're forgiven because you called me babe. Now, hush."

Frankie closed his eyes for a moment and then raised his hands. He started moving them, waving back and forth. He could feel that rush, old and familiar. He hadn't done it in a very long time, but it was like getting back on the proverbial bike.

The water froze for a moment, crystalline and shimmering in the air. Then it began to dance. Slow, fast, in loops and figure eights, sparkling patterns that dazzled even Frankie, who'd seen it many times before.

The rain moved around them, soaring out far in trembling droplets and then drawing close again before he set it on a new course. The air inside his self-made bubble was damp still but filled with the rushing of warm wind and tiny misting particles of captured rain.

It was so pretty out there in the dark, water droplets shining only with the lights from the street and the park lanterns. Frankie couldn't believe how long it had been since he'd done this. It had always felt like he was in the middle of a diamond—in every direction it was more sparkling and beautiful than the last.

Addison spun around in their dry dome, laughing in utter childish delight. "It's gorgeous!"

"No one else in my family can do this. Not very useful, but…"

"*Amazing.*"

Addison came over and wrapped his arms around Frankie. He kissed him on the lips, little biting kisses on his jaw, a soft lick on his ear. Frankie lost concentration all together and let the rain fall on them with a soft giggle.

"You can't kiss me when I'm trying to pay attention."

"Yeah, that's how we ended up with laughing sauce, right?"

Frankie grinned. "Yeah."

Addison shivered.

"Are you cold?" Frankie asked. He was warm, but any large-scale charm usually made him sweat.

"Sort of. It's pretty wet out here."

Frankie slipped his hand into Addison's and laid his head on Addison's slightly higher shoulder. "You want me to make you hot cocoa when we get in?"

"What kind of hot cocoa?"

Frankie was confused until he saw the grin on Addison's face. *Oh. That's nice.* His stomach heated. He hadn't expected Addison to be playful like he was, to accept everything so seamlessly, to have a sexy wild streak that was hidden and gorgeous and hot as hell.

They ran, not even bothering to attempt cover, back for Addison's condo. Inside they stripped and made cocoa naked. Addison cuddled him from behind and kissed and licked until the cocoa nearly scalded in the pan. Frankie charmed it with desire and a bit of naughtiness. The second wasn't his fault. He happened to be concentrating when Addison's hand slipped around to cup his growing erection.

When the cocoa was done and poured into cups, they took it to bed, where they sipped and kissed and tasted chocolate and each other's skin until the cocoa was long forgotten and they were locked together in the darkness with the wet rushing patter of the rain streaming through the open window.

Afterward, when their breathing had calmed, and the pounding rain with it, they slept, all tangled and curled and twined around each other, like if they got close enough their skin might just bond together.

THE MORNING WAS MET with shy happy smiles and small kisses. They cuddled in the wet morning light with the window open and birds chirping cheerily even through a misty drizzle. Addison stretched their hands up into the air and twined their fingers so closely that they looked like something else entirely: one being instead of two.

It was right then, in the new morning and the warmth of Addison's bed, that Frankie realized he knew for sure. He was in love with Addison, and not the vision with the house on the beach and the cute dog, but the real Addison. The one who was still a little uptight but possibly the sweetest guy Frankie had ever met, the one who was learning what it was like to really be with someone.

Frankie saw the happy surprise in Addison's eyes every time they took another step closer to a real relationship. It warmed his heart.

He reached up to toy with a wheat-colored wave of Addison's hair and sighed before he realized how silly and lovesick he probably looked.

Oh, well. In for a penny, in for a pound, right?

Addison squeezed him closer and smiled. "Do you want to sleep a while longer?" he asked.

"Sure," Frankie replied with a smile. He knew he wouldn't; he was still energized from his spell the night before, but it would be nice to hold Addison for a while. "Let's go back to sleep."

~

"DON'T YOU EVER WORK ANYMORE?" Frankie asked with a laugh.

Addison could tell he was just teasing, so he smiled. "I just got done with lunch at Fuego." He slung his bag onto the floor of the kitchen and flopped down onto his customary stool. He marveled again at how casual he felt with Frankie.

"And?" Frankie looked immediately interested. Addison supposed he'd always be interested in a critic's opinion of his competition.

He shrugged. "Not horrible. Good spices, good use of cheese."

"Good use of cheese? What the hell does that mean?"

Addison laughed. "I don't know what I meant," he answered. "I guess I thought I'd see if you were really listening."

"Of course I was listening. It was about food." Frankie gave him that crazy gorgeous smile that he loved so much. Addison couldn't help scooting his stool closer and wrapping his arms around Frankie's waist so he could nuzzle into his chest.

Frankie chuckled. "Some of us are working here." But he pulled Addison closer and dropped a kiss on his head so Addison didn't take him too seriously.

"What's for lunch? It smells awesome."

"Baked pasta primavera — fire-roasted veggies, cream sauce with brie and herbs, orecchiette pasta. Oh, and cheesy rosemary-garlic bread."

"What's orecchiette?"

"It's just a shape. It means little ears."

Addison made a face. "It sounded good before that fun fact."

Addison had settled in happily and was busily stealing chunks of tomato when his phone rang, chirping and vibrating in his pocket. He hoped it wasn't work calling him in to do some menial task. He tugged the phone out and flinched. It was worse.

Julia.

Addison hit the ignore button as quickly as he could and shoved the phone back into his pocket.

"Who was that, babe?" God, he loved when Frankie called him that. Still, guilt sank in his stomach hard.

"No one."

It was over. He'd ended it—more than once. He wasn't cheating on Frankie, not with his heart or anything else, but Julia didn't seem to get the picture.

In the past week and a half, he'd tried to tell her three different times that it wasn't going to happen, that they weren't going out socially and he was in an actual relationship, not just some dumb boy-on-the-side situation.

Situation.

That was the word she kept using for it. "We'll work out this situation," she said. It made him want to scream. He didn't want to confess to Frankie that he'd been in a relationship when they'd first met, but he thought he should at least tell him that Julia existed. She just refused to go away no matter how many times he evaded her or outright told her he was with his boyfriend.

"Doesn't look like no one. You seem pissed."

Addison opened his mouth to explain the whole thing,

but then froze. He realized that he couldn't. Damn. "I'm just hungry. I didn't eat much at Fuego."

"Addison..."

"Sometimes I hate that you can read me so well." He needed to tell Frankie about Julia. The last secret he'd kept from his boyfriend hadn't broken them apart, but he was worried another one would.

"Yeah." Frankie ruffled his hair. "Hey, do you want to go to that wine bar again tonight? Meet Dom and his new boy toy?"

Addison was relieved, but a bit let down that Frankie wasn't going to push it any further. It would've been easier if Frankie had wheedled it out of him.

"Yeah, let's go. What's the new guy's name? I'd hate to call him Kenny."

In the month or so that he'd been with Frankie, Dom'd had a few different guys, and he and Frankie usually managed to meet them. It was weird to be back in the same boat of meeting another couple for a date. Addison waited to feel trapped, thought that he might start to feel like a sweater couple, but it didn't happen.

It was actually nice to be in public with Frankie, holding hands and showing people he was in love. Every day he learned more and more what it was to be in a real couple—not one that was just for show. He'd already introduced Frankie to some of his friends from work. They'd never even known Julia existed, so that wasn't much of an issue. It felt good.

Frankie hesitated. "Shit. I forgot. I'll introduce myself first."

"'Kay." Addison tilted his head up for a kiss. "Hey, one of the customers out there looked pretty stressed when I walked in. Can you do anything for that?"

Frankie snorted. "I'm not Xanax, you know."

"I know, but..." He wiggled his fingers like he'd seen Dom doing.

"Yeah, yeah. What table is she at?"

"The one underneath the blue flowered thingy."

"That's table eight."

Right when Frankie said that, Owen came rushing in. He usually looked at least mildly worried, but now he'd progressed to full-on panic.

"What's the matter?" Frankie didn't look too concerned.

"Bethany just called. She's not coming in. Like ever. Her boyfriend is moving to LA to start a band and she's going with him."

Frankie's mouth dropped open and he froze where he was standing. "You've gotta be kidding me. It's not crowded yet, but in an hour or so...*shit.*"

Addison took off his suit jacket. "Hey, I'll do it. If we can number the tables with tape or something, I'll be fine. Owen will have to help me with the pricing."

"Have you waited tables before?"

Addison grinned. "Not exactly, but I can figure it out, right?" He couldn't believe how quickly he jumped to try something new.

Frankie thought for about two seconds before he pointed to a rack in the corner. "Grab an apron."

The next few hours were chaotic, but the best time Addison had had in years. He bustled around to the tables, taking orders, grabbing plates, telling Frankie when he thought one of the customers needed an extra pick-me-up. That was his favorite part. He liked the idea of helping people without them even knowing about it. It felt good to see someone smile who'd been down when they first walked in the door. He could see why Frankie had started doing it.

By the time the restaurant closed after dinner he was exhausted and grinning and ready to pass out and take on the world at the same time.

"You still up for the bar? That was a long afternoon for you."

Addison nodded. "My feet are killing me but I could use a glass of wine. Plus I like it when you're tipsy." He flashed a grin at Frankie.

"Yeah, I'm easy when I've had a few." Frankie chuckled and gave Addison a long, lingering kiss that was both sleepy and totally hot at the same time.

"I might be, too. You never know." Addison couldn't believe he'd just said that. He hadn't thought about bottoming in years, but the thought of it made his skin heat up all of a sudden.

"Really?" Frankie's face broke into a big grin.

"Yeah. I think so."

Addison was surprised with another long, deep kiss. "Damn, you're hot," Frankie panted when they'd finally come up for air.

"C'mon, babe. Let's go get some wine with Dom."

Frankie smiled and held out his hand.

CHAPTER ELEVEN

Frankie smiled at Dom and the new date, Terry. Showered and dressed, they'd made it to the wine bar in time to be seated in one of the cozy corner booths. Addison had his arm around him, and they were cuddled close on the bench. He kept getting teasing looks from Dom, who even stuck his finger in his mouth and gagged once when Addison kissed him on the nose.

He didn't mind being corny. It was weird because usually he'd push someone away if they tried to be so touchy in public. *Must just be love*, he thought. He'd realized sometime in the past week that he'd never really been in love before. That "can't stand not to be touching him" feeling was something completely new.

He was on his second glass of wine and feeling pretty good. He knew if he had another, he'd be well on his way to the point where he would tell people his family secrets and profess his love for Addison in sonnet form in front of the whole bar. Probably best to tell Addison in private first. No more wine for him.

"Hey, you want to go home?" Addison's whisper was

paired with a not-so-private nibble on his ear. Frankie shivered hard.

"Yeah. I want you inside of me. Right now." Frankie didn't realize how loud he said that until Dom and his date gawked at him.

Addison laughed and gathered Frankie close, grabbing his jacket at the same time. "I think I should get this one home."

Dom snickered. "Yes, you should. Apparently he needs to go to bed."

Frankie tried to glare at Dom as they slipped out of the booth. He wasn't sure if he was successful. Probably not, because he ended up almost tripping. But Addison managed to get him into his jacket, and by the time Frankie had his hand in the back pocket of Addison's jeans walking down the street, he felt tons better. He had a pleasant burn in his belly, and he was walking home with his man. Things were pretty damn nice.

"Love you, Addie," he murmured into the arm of Addison's jacket.

Addison stopped in the middle of the sidewalk and turned to face him. "Say that again."

Frankie's already-warm skin got even hotter. "I said I love you, didn't I?" He moaned and covered his face with his hands. "Oh, Jesus. This is so not how I planned this moment. Shit, I'm a jerk."

"Hey." Addison's warm hands came up to cup his face. "Stop it. I love you too, and this moment is perfect."

"Yeah?" Frankie swayed but soon righted himself.

"Of course. The last month and a half has changed my life. *You've* changed my life."

"Was it so bad before?"

Addison shrugged. "Boring. I did what my mother said

to do pretty much all the time. I was never what you'd call happy. Not like now."

"When do I get to meet this mother of yours? You met mine."

Addison groaned and hugged Frankie close. "Can we please not talk about her? It's been such an amazing night."

Frankie's belly heated up. "It could get a lot more amazing for both of us if you take me the rest of the way home."

By the time they got to the front door of Addison's condo, the wine had worn off a little. Even though Frankie had barely any tolerance, the buzz usually died pretty quickly, which was good.

"I love your place," Frankie murmured. He'd spent so many nights there lately, and with the warm wood floors, the pale-green walls, large comfortable furniture—it felt like home. His tiny apartment never had.

"I love you in my place," Addison responded. It seemed like he wanted to say more, but he didn't, just kissed Frankie and peeled his jacket off to drape it over the couch. "I just love you."

"Mmm. Love you too. Take me to bed?"

"Of course. Come, love."

Frankie's heart constricted at that. He had to make a joke so he didn't get teary eyed. "I will be. Multiple times."

Addison chuckled and pinched him on the butt. "Go on up, smarty pants. I'm going to get us some water. Be naked when I get there."

Frankie grinned and scampered up the stairs, pulling at the buttons on his shirt and jeans. Clothes thankfully off, he dove onto the bed that was almost his as much as it was Addison's by that point and went digging in the drawer for lube and condoms. He had them in his hand and was shutting the drawer when he felt the bed move. Addison had flopped down naked, hair rumpled and lips wet from the water he'd put on the dresser.

Frankie held out his hand. "C'mere."

Addison crawled over until he was looming on top of Frankie, knee nudging Frankie's legs apart. "Love you in my bed," he murmured, dropping kisses down Frankie's chest and sucking on a nipple. "Love you in my house."

"I love it here too." Frankie gasped when Addison got to his cock and sucked it in. Addison moaned delightfully. Frankie couldn't remember it feeling so good with anyone else.

"So stay," Addison said, coming up for air.

"I'm not going anywhere. I'll be here in the morning." Frankie pulled Addison up to kiss him. He needed to kiss him. He needed a whole lot of things that didn't include talking. Addison pulled away from him. Frankie tried to focus on his face instead of the lust that was clawing through him.

"No, love. Stay. I know it's only been...I just...I know we're right." He dropped his forehead onto Frankie's chest. "Just stay."

Wait, was he asking Frankie to move in? Really?

"You mean it?" It was awfully soon, Frankie knew, but still everything he'd wanted since he touched Addison and saw his future. They *were* right for each other. He knew it too.

Addison nodded and kissed his chest.

"Then, yes, I'll stay. I love you."

"I love you, too." Addison hesitated. "Will you make love to me?"

Frankie had been lifting his hips, trying to get closer to Addison's erection. He stalled. "Really?"

"Yeah." Addison rolled them over so Frankie's leg was sprawled across his thighs.

"Have you bottomed before?"

"In college, which was about a million years ago."

"But you liked it?"

"Yeah, I liked it. I'm better at being on top, at least I was back then, but I want it with you."

Frankie grinned and reached for the lube. "This is gonna be fun."

He kissed Addison long and deep, reveling in a taste so perfect that no recipe could come close to replicating it. He dropped the lube next to him on the covers and concentrated on touching Addison. His skin was silky on the inside of his thighs. Frankie licked at the tender softness and moaned.

Addison let his legs fall apart even further, encouraging Frankie's touch. "Please..." was all he said.

"What do you want, babe?"

Addison reached for one of Frankie's hands and guided it to his entrance. "Touch me."

"I'll do even better than that."

It wasn't something that Frankie did often, only once or twice before, but with Addison things were different. He wanted to feel everything he could feel, taste everything he could taste. Frankie licked and kissed his way up Addison's inner thighs, suckled the wrinkled skin of his balls, and licked into his crease to taste the skin of his entrance.

Addison choked out a garbled moan and grasped Frankie's shoulder. Frankie smiled to himself and then reached one hand up to toy with a nubby nipple while he slowly worked Addison open with his tongue.

Addison gripped his own cock and squeezed hard. "Baby, oh god, oh damn, I'm gonna come. Stop. *Stop*."

Frankie lifted his head and grinned. He slicked up his fingers. First one, then two delved into Addison's tight heat. He ate Addison's groans and kissed him with wet swipes of his tongue. Frankie could barely control his hand; Addison was bucking and moaning and losing control.

It was hot as hell.

Gone was the reserved newspaper writer who needed the help of wine to lose his inhibitions. In his place was a gorgeous glowing creature lost in his own pleasure.

"You ready?" Frankie whispered.

"Yeah," Addison answered with a gulp. "I want you."

Frankie hastily rolled on a condom and slicked himself up with lube. He paused at Addison's entrance, oddly shaky and unsure. "I love you," he whispered.

It was one of those moments in life when everything changes. Before, they could have left each other, gone their separate ways, and it would have hurt, sure, but it wouldn't have been impossible. Once Frankie sank inside of Addison, he'd be there forever, and Addison would be inside of him too. For the rest of his life. He didn't know why, or how he knew it was true, but it was. It was a sobering thought.

This guy is everything...

"I love you too, baby." Addison lifted his thighs to hug Frankie's flanks. "Inside. I want to feel you."

Frankie pushed and slowly entered the tight heat that was his future. It was dizzying and gorgeous, hot and perfect. He moaned. "You feel amazing."

"So do you." Addison hitched his hips closer to Frankie. "It's so...so good."

He moaned then and rolled his hips hard. Frankie leaned forward and kissed him, slowly starting to move his own hips. Addison wrapped one arm around Frankie, and with the other, he reached back and grabbed hold of the bottom of his headboard.

"More," Addison moaned. "Please."

Frankie felt like he was going to come apart at the seams, ripped in two by pleasure. He stroked harder, aiming for the place that would make Addison lose his mind.

"*Ohh*," he moaned. "Like that?"

"Yes. Perfect." Addison's voice was hoarse and breathless, debauched and beautiful. "I love you so much."

"Love you too." Frankie slung Addison's knees over his shoulders and bent forward. Addison gasped and grabbed his cock.

"I'm gonna come," he moaned, and stroked himself furiously. Frankie was on the edge too, shivering and quaking, gritting his teeth so he didn't lose control.

Frankie joined hands with Addison, and they stroked together until he shuddered hard and covered his stomach with warm release. The look on Addison's face was enough to make Frankie lose the control he'd been barely hanging on to. He might have blacked out for a minute. It was hard to tell. When he opened his eyes, Addison was below him, dragging breath into his lungs and grinning.

"Holy Jesus," Frankie said hoarsely. In those few amazing minutes, every missing piece of his universe, even ones he'd never known he missed, had slid quietly into place. And it all had to do with the one perfect man who was lying beneath him with a dreamy smile and sweat glossed skin.

"You're telling me," he answered.

Yeah. Addison wasn't going anywhere.

~

"DID YOU HEAR SOMETHING DOWNSTAIRS?" Frankie rolled over and propped his head sleepily on Addison's chest.

Addison listened for noises coming from the first floor. "I don't hear anything. Good morning, by the way."

"Mmm, morning." Addison was treated to a long kiss. "Do you still love me in the harsh light of day, or was that all the wine talking?"

Addison couldn't help but chuckle. "I should ask you the same thing. I was pretty sober by the time we got here. You, on the other hand, were..." A deep blush crept up his chest onto his face. Last night had been so damn hot. He couldn't wait to try it again and again. He'd have to wait a while though because he was a bit sore but—

"Addison Albright, I know you're here. Quit trying to pretend you're asleep so you can avoid me."

Oh, shit shit shit.

Frankie sat up. "Who's that?"

"That," Addison drawled sarcastically, "is my mother." He jumped up and scrambled around the bed for his boxers.

Frankie chuckled. "She's not going to come up here, is she?"

Addison found his boxers at the bottom of the bed and tried unsuccessfully to jam his legs into them for a few moments before he managed to drag them on. "I wouldn't put it past her. She has before."

He hopped up and jogged toward his bedroom door so he could intercept her before she—*Aw, damn.*

His bedroom door burst open. He tried to block it, but she barged right in. "It's nearly ten, Addison, why aren't you—"

She screamed. Addison jumped himself, forgetting for the moment that he was still nearly naked. She screamed again and backed toward the door. "What in the good Lord's name are you doing with that...that..."

"He's a man, mother. This is Frankie. He's my boyfriend. And I'm reminded of why I didn't tell you in the first place."

"But you're engaged! To Julia. You're not gay."

Addison turned in time to see Frankie's mouth drop open and his eyes go wide. "You're engaged? To a woman?"

"No, babe, it's not like that." Addison wished he had the perfect words.

"Yes, it is!" his mother countered. "Her name is Julia and she would be crushed if she saw this *display*."

"Julia knows all about me and Frankie, mother." *Oh, shit, that didn't come out right.*

"Julia? There really is a fiancée?" Frankie leapt out of bed and started yanking clothes on. "So what, you and her are playing a game? She's okay with this? You have an arrangement because she knows you like dick? What is it?" He paused, looking back and forth from panicked Addison to his horrified mother. "You know what—I don't want to know. I'm gone."

Frankie ran down the stairs and headed for the front door. Addison was about to run after him when he realized he was still embarrassingly unclothed. He scrambled for his jeans, glaring at his mother the whole time, and then went sprinting after Frankie. Of course he missed him.

Damn it. Son of a bitch.

He jogged back into his condo to get dressed and go after Frankie, only to find his mother sitting placidly on the couch.

"Mother, I broke up with Julia weeks ago, she's just not taking no for an answer."

"Why should she? She's your fiancée."

Addison sighed. "I'm gay, Mom. Gay. I'm not going to marry Julia. If Frankie will still take me after what just happened, I'm hoping to spend the rest of my life with him. I love him."

She rolled her eyes. "You don't know what you want, which is why Julia and I have to tell you all the time."

And with that he remembered every moment of his old life that he never wanted to live again. Addison pointed toward the door. "Get. Out. I expect you to leave your key on the counter. You will be returning, with invitation only, after I've begged the man I love to come back and explained that you didn't know what the hell you were talking about."

"Don't be ridiculous, Addison. You're acting like a child."

"No, for once I'm acting like a man." He went over and pulled her up by the elbow. He didn't do it forcefully, although at that moment it would have felt good. "I said out. And give me my key."

"You don't really love that boy. It's only a silly phase, probably from living in this *neighborhood*." She gestured out the window with pursed lips.

Addison grabbed her key ring himself and pulled his house key off of it. With any luck, it would soon belong to Frankie. Never hers again.

"Mother, you don't have a clue who I am at all."

Then he escorted her quickly to the front door, shut it behind her, and locked it after she'd gone.

CHAPTER TWELVE

Frankie's head hurt like the devil. He wasn't sure if it was from the wine or—no, it wasn't the wine. A hangover wasn't even part of the culprit for the god-awful hammering ache that was splitting his head apart and settling gelatinously in his stomach.

He felt like hell, and every time he thought of Addison and the look of absolute guilty horror that dawned on his face, he wanted to scream. It was true. That look said it all. So no, not the wine. Not at all.

He'd felt so wonderful earlier, when they'd first woken up. He'd been all full of love, wrapped in his man's arms. There had been pictures in his head of the future, living with Addison in his homey condo, them kissing in the restaurant's kitchen while he tested new recipes.

Not anymore. The only thing in his head was pounding and a tightness that led to this shooting pain that zapped him behind his ear every few seconds.

He'd dragged himself into his apartment fifteen minutes ago, sat on the couch despondently, and stared at his unadorned walls. He couldn't think about what he was going to do next, how he was going to drag himself to work the next day, how he was going to keep on walking and eating and even someday trying to find someone new. The idea felt so wrong. Everything felt wrong. He slumped further into the couch.

I'm not going find anyone new. If this is love, it sucks. I'm done.

He picked up his phone to call Sofia, which had become his reflex lately. They'd been friendly when he was still back at home, but the distance from his family had somehow made the two of them far closer.

"Hey, Sof." Frankie sighed into the phone. He knew his cousin, and she could probably already tell something was very, very wrong.

"Hi. What's up?" Her voice sounded weird. Like maybe she was trying not to be overheard.

"What's up with you? You sound weird."

"Oh, uh. Nothing. Hold on." He heard a door close and then Sofia came back to the phone. "You okay?"

"Not really. I guess I was wrong about Addison. He's engaged. To a chick."

Sofia was silent for a few moments. "You weren't wrong. I can't tell what's going on. Do you want me to come there?"

"I just want him back. I want this morning to have never—"

"*Frankie.*"

Too late. He heard a voice on the other end of the phone, muffled but still discernible. "Is that my son on the phone?"

"Yes, auntie." Sofia, like the rest of them, probably figured it was no good to lie. Frankie's mom would know the truth anyway and it was better not to annoy her.

Shit.

Frankie hadn't even taken a breath when there was a feeling, that woosh in his belly that told him she was there. In his apartment. Fantastic.

"I told you so." Her voice was strident and a bit smug. "I didn't even have to get it out of Sofia. I could see it all over her face."

Frankie groaned. He reached for the couch throw to pull over his head. "I'm not going to tell you to leave. You don't listen anyway. Just get it over with."

She smiled at him, soft and motherly. It was creepy. "Now that you're done with your boring newspaper man, why don't you come home?"

Oh. Now he saw what she was up to. "Not going to happen, Mother."

"Why won't you give Laurent a chance? He's been asking about you again."

Frankie rolled his eyes. Ouch. That hurt. He massaged his temples gently. She really was never going to give him a break.

"Mom, why can't you just leave me alone? I love being a chef. It makes me happy when my food makes other people happy. I like it here. I'm not coming home, I'm not going to join your society people, and I'm not going to do anything with Laurent. Ever."

She gritted her teeth but still managed to maintain a smile. Impressive. "We do own that building in the French Quarter. You can open a restaurant there. It's not too far to the city."

Oh, that was a new tactic. He had to give her points for concession. Still not going to happen.

"I like it here, Mother. End of story."

"You want to stay here to be with your boyfriend who's engaged to a woman?"

The stabbing lightning pain hit him again, hard and fast behind his ear. "I don't want to talk about him."

It hurt so bad. Not just the headache but everywhere. The thought of Addison touching someone else made him want to vomit. Frankie's pocket vibrated. He pulled out his phone.

Addison. Of course.

There was that awful pain again. He went to silence it, but he couldn't.

Am I really that weak?

It wasn't weakness, he told himself. It was love, right? Didn't Addison deserve a chance to explain?

No. He's engaged.

But if Addison was calling maybe there was more to the story. Frankie didn't think Addison was the kind of guy who would tell someone he loved him if he didn't mean it. He tried to imagine Addison being the kind of guy who would run any scam that well. There was no way. Addison wasn't *that* guy.

Frankie went to open his phone.

"Oh, I don't think so." His mother shot out her hand and wrapped long fingers around his wrist.

There was a jolt that forced him to drop his phone. It bounced on his couch once before sliding to the floor. Then there was a moment of disorienting black. The next thing he knew, he was sprawled out on the floor of his parents' house, all the damn way in Vieux Chene, Louisiana.

Now that was some *bullshit*.

"Damn it, Mother! Take me back." Frankie scrambled to his feet. He hated how he felt like a little awkward duck every time he was in his family's presence. His annoying brother Jean had once said that even the maids had more power than him.

His mother swiped an invisible dust bunny off of his shirt. "Take yourself back." She chuckled. "Oh, that's right. You can't."

Frankie was pissed. There was no more dignified word for it. "I'm sure you don't mean to be a big bitch, not to mention a kidnapper, so I'm going to give you the benefit of the doubt. Take me back to my apartment."

He was about two seconds away from stomping out the door and finding Sofia. But the reality was, he didn't know if Sofia was capable of making the jump with him in tow.

"I don't want to be here. Take me *back*."

"Why? So you can answer the phone when that reporter calls again? And he will. He'll probably try to convince you that he's done with her and he only loves you. It's the oldest story in the book, Frankie. I'm not going to have a Vallerand fall for it. We'll look like fools. You know I can't stand that."

Frankie sputtered. "Addison and I have nothing to do with you and it's not your choice to make. But of course I'm stuck here since you didn't let me get my wallet before you took me hostage."

His mother ignored him, as usual. It was so damn infuriating. "Quit being so dramatic, Francois." She craned her neck toward the living room entrance. "Ah, *Jean*. I'm glad you're here. And Laurent. Thank you for coming on such short notice."

His brother and the cool sophisticated Laurent entered through the doorway, instead of materializing like he would've expected them to.

Fucking hell. Like he needed more witnesses to his humiliation. Annoyed didn't come close to covering it anymore. Pissed didn't either. What game was she playing?

"Hello, Francois, it's nice to see you again." Laurent gracefully extended his pale hand for shaking.

Everything about the man, from his artfully tailored slacks and button-up to his perfectly manicured hair, annoyed Frankie. But he had to be polite. *Damn it.*

He reached out and clasped Laurent's hand in his own.

At that moment, both his brother and his mother covered their joined hands, sending a surge of energy swirling black, painful, and shrieking through him. His consciousness was battered by the energy for long seconds—then nothing. Frankie yanked his hand back and stumbled along the oriental rug until he came in contact with a divan, and he sat with a clunk.

"What the hell did you guys just do?" His head was spinning, and his vision was blurred around the edges. He imagined this was what getting shocked felt like, but perhaps less pleasant.

"They didn't do anything," Laurent said quietly. "It didn't work." Laurent turned to Frankie's mother. "He's been bonded already. A true bond."

His mother's jaw dropped, and Jean looked oddly relieved.

Frankie flattened himself against the divan as far away from his family and Laurent as he could get. "What the *hell.* You tried to bond me to him? Those are nearly impossible to break."

"Yes," Laurent said slowly. "You were one of my potential mates, but clearly I am not one of yours. You have already been bonded to your lover."

"Addison?" God, what a mess. He'd managed to accidentally magically attach himself to his engaged boyfriend. Of course. What the hell was he supposed to do?

"Yes," Laurent confirmed. "Addison, if that's his name. Did you not mean to do it?"

Frankie winced. Of course not. He wasn't that talented.

"That's impossible!" His genteel aristocratic mother screeched like a banshee. "That man is engaged to a woman and he's a nobody." Frankie wondered which was worse in her eyes.

"You know that's not true, Mother." It was the first time Jean had spoken.

"What's not true? That he's a nobody? By Vallerand standards it's most certainly true."

"No, it's the other."

"Just spit it out, Jean. I've got a long walk ahead of me." Frankie rolled his eyes at him like the bratty younger brother he was. He had no intention of doing anything as ridiculous as walking. Jean probably would have rolled his eyes right back if he wasn't so intent on getting his point across.

"He's not still with that woman, Frankie. His mother was misinformed. Think. You have to be able to tell that you have his whole heart. You've bonded with him, Frankie. That wouldn't be possible if he'd split his affections with another."

"Jean Luc Vallerand. Shut it," their mother growled. It was ugly to say the least. Jean didn't seem to be impressed. Of course, he'd been dealing with her a lot more years than Frankie.

"Mother, quit interfering. It's not going to do any good and you'll get more wrinkles." Jean gave her a dismissive wave. Frankie swore he could see the steam coming from her head. "Here, Frankie." Jean held out his hand.

"What are you going to do to me?"

"Take you back to where you belong."

That was all Frankie needed to hear. He grabbed Jean's hand and felt a momentary yank. As easy as that, he was in his living room, backing up and falling onto his couch, where his phone still sat open.

"I can't believe you..." He looked up at his brother askance.

"I'm not always an asshole, Frankie. And I know a bit about loving someone and not getting to be with them."

Frankie's eyes widened. "Who?"

Jean winced but then shook his head. "It doesn't matter, does it? I need to get back to my family. Best of luck, little brother."

And with a small tremor, much cleaner than their mother's dramatic jolt, Jean was gone.

CHAPTER THIRTEEN

Not ten seconds after Jean left, Frankie felt another pop and Sofia was standing in his apartment looking about as sorry as one person who didn't do anything wrong could look.

"I can't believe that happened," she said. "I'm so sorry."

Frankie scoffed. "You can't control what my mom overhears. Nor can you stop her from being a gigantic pain in my ass."

"Did they really bond you to Laurent?" Sofia's voice was about as horrified as Frankie had felt back home when he figured out what they wanted to do.

"No. They couldn't. Not because they didn't try, though. I can't fucking believe my mom."

"What do you mean, they couldn't? I thought the whole point was that Laurent felt the potential of a bond with you."

Frankie spit out a humorless laugh. "He did. The irony of this whole day is I'm already bonded. Seems like I can't control that any more than I could control bonding to that damn spoon."

"Addison?"

"Obviously. This is such a mess."

His cousin shook her head vehemently. "No, he's right for you. It's going to be okay, Frankie. I promise."

Frankie sighed and then nodded. "I believe you. It's just going to take me a minute to get past today. In lots of ways."

"I know. But he loves you and you love him. It's the only thing that matters." Sofia cupped his face and then gave him a quick kiss on the cheek. "I'm going back home but let me know if you need to talk. I'll be here in a heartbeat."

"Thanks, Sof."

With a delicate pop, Sofia was gone and he was alone in his apartment. Frankie wandered around inside his apartment for nearly an hour before he gained enough equilibrium to check his phone.

Addison. Five times.

His message light was blinking. Frankie dialed his voice mail.

"Baby, my mom was wrong. I'm not with her anymore. Not since we first met. I love you. Please answer." Addison's voice sounded frantic and upset. There was another message. "I need to talk to you. I'm sorry. Please?" Frankie couldn't bring himself to erase the messages, although the hurt in Addison's voice made his gut clench. There was one more. "I'm coming over there. I won't give up. I meant what I said. I want us forever, Frankie. I love you…"

Frankie hit redial. He was ending this stupid thing right away. Addison loved him, he loved Addison…Addison wasn't picking up his phone? Frankie got voicemail.

"Addie, babe. I know. I know you aren't with her. I'll tell you how, just call me back. I love you. I'm sorry I believed your mom."

He stumbled into his cold bedroom. It held none of the

appeal of Addison's, with that big warm bed that smelled just like Addison and the bright windows and golden wood floors. He lay down on his own bed, the one he'd barely been on in the last few weeks, and curled up with his phone against his chest. He'd just lie there for a while, until Addison got his message and called him back. Surely Addison would call him back. Surely.

Frankie woke up in his dark apartment. He'd been asleep for two hours. He checked his phone but he had no missed calls and his stomach clenched violently. Where was Addison? Frankie lurched into his bathroom and threw up. *Is this what bonding feels like?* Would he react like this every time they got in a fight? He sure as hell hoped not. As much as he loved Addison, they were bound to get pissy once in a while. Frankie washed out his mouth and grabbed his keys. He had to go find Addison.

He was surprised when a cold sleeping body fell over the threshold into his hallway. Frankie's breath caught in his throat.

"Addie! How long have you been out here?" He dragged a rather stunned-looking Addison into the apartment, dropping kisses over his face.

"Um, this morning? I don't know how long," Addison said groggily.

His poor baby looked tired and stiff.

"Come inside and lie down. I'm going to put you to bed for a while." Frankie rubbed at Addison's hands. "You're freezing!"

"Frankie," he mumbled. "So glad you're home. I'm sorry. Love you." Addison's voice was thin and tired.

"It's okay. Just come and sleep."

"I wasn't engaged. Not anymore. She just wouldn't leave me alone. I told her..."

Frankie helped Addison into his bed, nowhere near as soft and wonderful as Addison's but so much better now that Addison was in it. He tugged covers over his shivering boyfriend and kissed him on the forehead.

"I know. I'm sorry I didn't trust you at first. It just sounded so..."

"Believable?" Addison rolled over and opened his eyes all the way. "I wouldn't do that to you. I love you, not her. *You.*"

Addison held the covers up in invitation. Frankie crawled under with him, jeans and all. "What happened with you and your fiancée...Julia?"

"Good memory."

Frankie huffed out a mirthless chuckle. "I doubt I'll forget much about this morning for a long time. So, truth. What happened?"

Addison shrugged. "I'm gay, or at least slightly bi with a *very* strong lean in the male direction."

"That I know. How did you end up engaged to a woman if you're not very interested in them?"

"It was easier than having the conversation a million times."

"What conversation?"

"The one where all her friends were married and she hated being single and basically we looked good together and she liked to put us in matching sweaters."

Frankie choked. "You're not serious. You *can't* be serious."

"Yeah. A few of her couple friends have matching everything—same pants, same sweaters, same cars."

"Why bother? It's like being with yourself. How boring."

"That's what I thought. I rarely said it out loud though. That tended to get me in trouble."

"And you broke up with her for me?"

"For myself really. But, yeah, because I met you. I wanted to fall in love, for real, not in matching-sweater land. I wanted what I saw..."

Frankie kissed him to bring him back. "What you saw where?"

"I was on the way into my place one night and I saw these two guys on a stoop kissing like they couldn't breathe without each other's lips. I wanted that for myself, if only just one time."

"And that's where I came along."

"Yeah, but one time wasn't enough. I wanted it again and again and then I wanted it always."

Frankie remembered what Addison had asked him the other night.

Stay...

"You still want me to move in? Even after yesterday?"

Addison slid his hands under Frankie's shirt and pulled it over his head. He kissed Frankie's face, his neck, the thin skin of his eyelids. "How could I not?"

FRANKIE WOKE up early the next morning to the sound of Addison arguing on the phone. He was trying to do it softly, Frankie could tell, but even on the other side of the bathroom door he heard the mumble of the conversation get louder until Addison stalked out of the bathroom and threw his phone down. On the bed of course, so he didn't break it. He flopped down and sighed.

"Mother?"

Addison gave Frankie a wry grin. "How'd you know?"

"You've got a horrible case of Mom face."

"Mom face, huh? You probably won't have to deal with that for a while."

Frankie grimaced. "After what happened in Louisiana, she's going to be lying low for a long time. I think Jean probably ripped into her pretty good when he got back from dropping me off here." He'd given Addison a short sketch of what had happened the day before. Details—well, he was saving those for later.

"I still can't believe that. You went to Louisiana, argued with your mom, almost got married, argued with her some more, were rescued by Jean and back here in, what? A few hours?"

"I didn't *almost* get married. I couldn't have."

"What do you mean?"

"Well," Frankie hedged. Apparently later had come. "There's this thing that happens when a witch chooses a mate. They can only do it with a few potential people, and I, um, did it accidentally but..."

"Frankie. What?"

"I bonded myself to you, okay? I didn't mean to do it without your permission, I don't even know when it happened but when Laurent went to bond himself to me he said he couldn't. He could feel that I'd already bonded with someone else. *You.*"

Frankie flinched. It wasn't every day that a person finds out they got accidentally married, and Addison wasn't the best with change. He was surprised by the big grin he got followed by a long, sweetly sloppy kiss.

"Does that mean you're mine forever? You can't get rid of me?"

Frankie nodded. "I guess technically, we could date other people if it came to that, but I can't bond with anyone else, and if you ever met another witch, you couldn't bond with them either. That much is permanent. It won't, um, feel like this with anyone else."

"I don't want it to." Addison kissed him again. "And I like permanent. Especially if it comes with you." Frankie couldn't help giving him another long kiss. Addison finally pulled back. He looked a bit nervous. "So I have a confession too. That was my mother on the phone."

"Yeah, I know." *Not much of a confession.*

"Um, well, she's coming over here for dinner."

Frankie drew back. "Are you sure you want to do that, babe? It didn't go so well last time and I don't want you to get hurt if she disapproves still. You know that's likely."

"I know. She's my only family and I have to try. I think I kind of shook her up yesterday when I yelled at her. She seems...a little different. Maybe more ready to at least admit that you and I aren't a figment of my imagination." Addison paused. "So you're not mad about dinner?"

"'Course not. She's your mother and I've been disapproved of my whole life by my own family anyway. I'm used to it. I just want you to be happy."

"With you around, I doubt that will be a problem."

"THAT'S IT!" Frankie plopped the last box of his stuff on Addison's dining room table. Not just Addison's anymore. His too. It had been a hell of a two weeks, working, packing, throwing away useless crap he'd accumulated. It was worth it.

"Addison?" His voice rang in the empty condo. That's when he saw the note.

Welcome home, baby! Today it's officially yours too. Ours. I went to the store to get some wine to celebrate. Be back in twenty. Love you.

—A

Frankie touched the corner of the letter with his finger, as if he could feel where Addison had held the paper down to write. It might have been sentimental of him, but he folded up the note and slipped it into his wallet—a memento of his first day living with Addison. He didn't plan to ever leave. His phone buzzed in his pocket.

"Do you want brie or gouda for the crackers?" Addison spoke without introduction. He didn't need one anymore. Frankie smiled. *Aww. Just like our first date.* It hadn't been that long ago, but it seemed like forever.

"Are you buying grapes too?" he teased.

Frankie could hear Addison's grin through the phone. "Green and red."

"You're a dork, but I love you. Get home. We've already got some wine to drink."

"Oooh, are you going to get out the good stuff?" Addison knew about Frankie's stash of fey wine. They kept it hidden in case of visitors. That wasn't something that regular folks needed to get into unawares.

"I'll get out the good wine and get a picnic blanket ready."

"Will you be naked?"

Frankie feigned shock. "It's still light out!"

"Naked. Ten minutes tops."

He chuckled. "Yessir."

. . .

THE FLOOR PICNIC was silly and romantic and the best way that Frankie could think of to celebrate moving in with the man he'd fallen so completely in love with. They fed each other grapes and drank strong fairy wine. Frankie lay with his head on Addie's chest, and they threaded and unthreaded their fingers, watching them glow in the light that crashed beautiful and startlingly pink through the window, bright from the setting sun.

Eventually they dragged themselves to bed and made love slower and sweeter than they ever had before. It felt like they were in it together forever. Frankie couldn't stand to believe otherwise. Sleep came easy and swift with his arms around Addison, his leg snuggled between Addison's muscular thighs. He whispered "I love you" against Addison's chest and felt, rather than heard, the low rumbling response. As he was drifting in that heavy half-sleep place, Frankie smiled to himself.

I'm here. I live here. It's real.

THAT NIGHT FRANKIE dreamt of a house by the ocean. There was breeze that blew in, soft and salty from the sea, a dog, and a white-and-blue coverlet. Him and Addison were cuddled under the coverlet laughing, kissing, and twining gold ringed left hands together in the sun. But the dream was different this time. Because instead of feeling like it was something that *could* be, perhaps, if all his stars lined up perfectly...it felt like something that would certainly come to pass.

In his sleep, Frankie smiled.

ABOUT MJ O'SHEA

MJ O'Shea has never met a music festival, paintbrush, or flower crown she can stay away from. She loves rainstorms and a perfect cup of tea, beach days, music, bright colors, and more than anything a cozy evening with a really great book.

She is from the Pacific Northwest. While she still lives there and loves it, MJ has the heart of a wanderer. So she puts all her dreams of far off places and extraordinary people in her books.

Except for every once in a while when she does what all travelers have to do on occasion... come home.

SNEAK PEEK OF A LITTLE TASTE OF MAGIC

Arlo Vallerand woke with a start and sat up in bed. It was bright outside his window, glowing with the soft warmth of a late summer morning in San Francisco. It took him a while to force himself into the real world. The edges of sleep still shimmered in the corners of his vision. They slowly mixed with the morning sun and disappeared, but they left Arlo with this feeling he couldn't quite surface from. Like Déjà vu, but somehow not.

He'd just had the most *realistic* dream. It was uncanny. And very unlike him.

... Snow and wind swirled outside, and the sound of laughter bubbled happily from the next room... His belly was warm and tingly. He'd never been so happy. Arlo smelled tomatoes and melting cheese. There was laughter in the distance and a warmth like he'd never felt in his life. Completion. Joy...

Arlo blinked a few times and tried to shake the dream, but he couldn't. The feelings were all still there – intense happiness, that inexplicable belly-deep sense of *rightness*, the laughter the smells, a voice calling his name. He still felt all of it. And he had no idea where the dream had come from.

The feeling welled up inside him, swallowed him whole, shimmered out of every pore. It was magic – the real forever kind.

"Baby. Are you done in there?"

It was a voice he knew somehow, but he couldn't remember it. He wanted to hear it again.

"Arlo? Babe? Let me help you. It'll be bedtime before that thing is ready to eat." The voice was accompanied by a soft chuckle.

Arlo tried to look up, but he couldn't. He couldn't see the face that went with the voice.

He needed to see a face...

Nothing in his life had felt more real, more necessary than the man in the dream, whoever he was.

He didn't know what to do with the dream. It really wasn't like him to dream much at all, let alone something that realistic. He felt drugged, but weirdly awake. Wired. It was too early to be up, but Arlo didn't think he was going to fall back to sleep. He flopped back down on his lovely bed, in his cousin's perfect little townhouse, and stared at the ceiling.

Even hours later, the intense longing for something he'd only seen in a dream wouldn't go away.

"Lasagnas are done, Frankie. You want me to work on the pastry dough?" Arlo leaned against the counter and watched his cousin move around the ancient, brick-walled kitchen.

He'd grown to love the old kitchen over the summer -

tall and cavernous but somehow homey. It usually smelled like baking bread and one of his cousin's specialties. The kitchen was rarely quiet, either. It was usually filled to the brim with chatter and clanking pots, noise from the dining area and even a radio that played bossa nova whenever his cousin's best friend stopped by to help.

"No, I want you to do the lasagnas." Frankie winked at him. "They were your idea. I want you to see it through to the end."

"I told you they were done," Arlo said. Frankie had to know that. Their smell was wafting on the air, filling the room.

"That's not what I meant," Frankie said. "I want you to *do* the lasagnas."

"Oh." Charm them. His cousin wanted him to charm them. "I don't think I'm ready to try it on food we're going to serve to customers."

"Pfft." Frankie rolled his eyes. "Sure you are. Hold your hand over the lasagna and concentrate. We're going to try infusing this one with just a light bit of happiness and sunshine. I'm sick of the rain."

Arlo took a deep breath and let it out slowly. *Here goes.* He tried to put last night's dream out of his mind. The same dream he had the night before...and the night before that. A voice, a feeling, crisp falling snow, and the smell of lasagna. There was a reason he'd changed the menu today. The dream had taken over his nights and most of his waking thoughts. It was impossible to push it aside.

He ignored the heavy summer rain that pounded on Cucina Capri's high windows and tried to pull in the warmth of the kitchen and the memory of yesterday's hazy glow until both things were nestled somewhere in his chest.

Then he remembered the voice in the dream, the happiness he'd felt and added that to the growing ball of light.

Arlo wanted to take that feeling and put it in the lasagna. Just that feeling. Nothing else. He concentrated on his cousin Frankie's voice and whispered, "Happiness. Warmth. Sunshine."

Arlo's palm tingled a bit and then he lifted his hand. Frankie clapped him on the back. "Good job. Take a taste and see if it worked."

Arlo dipped a spoon – not his cousin's treasured wooden one, of course – into sauce that had pooled at the corner and tasted it. He was immediately filled with a faint but pleasant sensation of golden light, baking bread, the coziness that came from Frankie's cooking, warmth, love, and, closeness too. It mellowed in his chest and made him smile.

"It worked."

He put the spoon down on the work surface and grinned. It had taken months to get where he was. When he'd first arrived in Cucina Capri's kitchen, he'd been a mess.

"You're getting so much better at that. You'd be surprised how hard an accurate food charm is for most of our family."

Arlo grinned. Sometimes he wondered how it was possible that Frankie was a cousin, rather than his brother. He sure seemed far more like Arlo than the rest of the Vallerands.

"Okay," Frankie said. "On the next pan, we're doing it without speaking out loud. Remember. Happiness and sunshine."

Arlo tried to protest, but Frankie held up his spoon like a sword. "I know you can do it. Don't be stubborn."

"I can only do it silently when I don't mean to."

"See? If you're doing it subconsciously, that means you're strong with emotion charms. I've never done it accidentally. At least not when I wasn't already in the middle of charming something." Frankie smiled and blushed a bit.

"Do I want to know?" Arlo asked. He knew his cousin had a very good relationship with his husband, Addison. *Very* good. He wasn't sure if he needed more details than he already had after nine months of living with them.

"Oh, it's nothing like that. Really. I was just in the middle of charming some fruit sauce once when Addie walked up and tickled me. I kind of gave my sauce the giggles. But I've never done it subconsciously from scratch. That's, like, a whole different level. I've never met a witch who could do that."

Arlo had to hold back his own snort. "You really gave fruit sauce the giggles. Wow."

"Please don't repeat that story back home." Frankie cringed and swept his dark hair off his face – a gesture Arlo found they had in common. "If my mom doesn't already know, I'd rather save myself the humiliation."

Frankie's mom was a bit.... interesting to say the least. A purist. Old school. Honestly, she was a snobby pain in the ass. Arlo didn't blame Frankie for moving across the country from Louisiana to get away from her. He also didn't blame him for wanting to hide his quirkier moments from her judgment.

"Lips sealed. Are we going to do the rest of the lasagnas before you open?" Arlo asked.

"Yes. Yes. And I'll do the cheesecakes. I think with ... openness. People could use a bit of interaction with each other, right?"

"Sure." Arlo grinned. After all these months, he still loved watching Frankie work.

"Since you've got the food charming down, you want to work on rain spells next? They're completely useless, but they'll impress the boys," Frankie said with a wink. "I should know."

"How could I say no to that?" Arlo chuckled.

~

I HAVE *to go find him.*

Arlo had just woken up again, heart racing, from another dream. The same voice, the same snow, five days in a row. It had to mean something. It *had* to.

Arlo pulled himself out of bed and stumbled to the closet. His chest ached a bit, like there had been something there and it was suddenly gone. He shook off the feeling and pulled his bags from the floor of the closet. He started to pack his belongings away. It wouldn't take long. He'd never had very many things. Arlo had to find whoever it was. He had to find the voice.

"Arlo? What are you doing?" His cousin Frankie stood in the doorway, scrubbing a hand through tousled dark curls that looked a lot like his own but a few inches shorter. He had on a pair of pajama pants and a tank top and looked confused. Arlo felt bad about waking him up.

"Sorry if I was being loud."

It was early, probably only a little bit past sunrise. Arlo knew he must look like he'd lost his mind, frantically packing in the pale light of early morning. He also knew that Frankie would understand.

Arlo had been staying with Frankie and his husband Addison in San Francisco since Christmas time, by far the longest he'd been *anywhere* since he'd left home. He'd loved his time with them, learning from Frankie and growing into his skills. He'd thought he might stay there with them. He'd been happy there, after all.

But now he had to go. He *needed* to go.

"That's okay." Frankie walked over and sank onto Arlo's bed. "Are you going to explain to me what's going on here?"

"I've been having dreams," Arlo said. *Okay, that sounded a little dramatic.* He shoved a shirt into his duffel bag.

"Fantastic attention to detail. You want to expand on that a little?" Frankie smiled tiredly.

"Don't be sarcastic," Arlo said. He pushed the heel of his hand against his eye for a moment. It didn't help ground him. "I'm too flustered to try bantering with you."

"Sorry. Tell me about the dreams."

"You know how Sofia has dreams? You know, *dreams*?" Arlo asked. That was enough of an explanation. He saw the moment Frankie got it, loud and clear on his face. Frankie's eyes widened slightly, and he bit his lip.

"Yeah. Of course, I know about her dreams," he rushed out. "Really?" Arlo and Frankie were both very aware of Arlo's sister's best skill. She'd had it for years, but prophetic dreams weren't a common gift in their family. The past few nights for Arlo had been a first. He wasn't going to act – dreams weren't his thing after all – but the dream just kept happening, over and over. Even Arlo wasn't that clueless.

"Yes. *Dream* dreams. Like hers. Or the same one over and over, I guess."

Frankie's eyes went wide. He stumbled into the room and sank down on Arlo's unmade bed. "Like..."

"I don't dream like Sofia does. At least, I never have before, but I have been. All week. And it feels real. Like something that's supposed to happen. I wake up every day and I can *still* feel it." He didn't know how to explain how it felt different, not like a normal dream. Or how he'd known that whatever was in the scene, those people, the smells, that *feeling*, was something he needed to find.

"You want to call your sister?" Frankie asked gently. Sofia would be able to help him, but talking to her wouldn't cure the itch under his skin. Wouldn't rid the need to find the person attached to the voice he could still hear in the back of his head. The one who called him baby, and felt like forever.

"Nah. I'm just going to get on the road. You know if we call, she'll come here and if she comes here, it's going to be a big *thing*, and I just..." He needed to go. Like, immediately.

"Babe." Frankie sighed. "Do you even know where you're going?"

Arlo knew his mother and Frankie had hoped living with a like-minded family member would cure him of his need to wander. He'd kind of hoped it would, too. And it had. Before the dream. Before the magnet that was pulling him out of San Francisco and towards the snow and the lasagna and that aching love that still pulsed in his chest.

"It was snowing in the dream. So north somewhere, I'd imagine. Probably east too."

"It's a pretty big country, man. That's not a lot to go on. I think you should call your sister."

Arlo stood silently for a few moments. And then he felt it right in his gut like he should've known all along. Zero doubt. "Maine," he said. "I'm going to Maine."

Maybe he did need to call Sofia. Dreams and visions were so out of his skill range, and he should make sure he wasn't doing something wrong. He'd call once he got on the road.

Frankie looked worried. "Maine's a long way from San Francisco."

Arlo nodded. "It is. I suppose I'd better get going."

~

THE TOWN OF BAXTER HOLLOW, Maine, hadn't changed much in the past hundred years or so and Gray Baxter quite liked it that way – as he should since it was his family who'd founded the town back in the pre-Revolutionary War days. Sure, cars and stoplights and typical day-to-day things had made their way in through Baxter Hollow's borders, but the streets still looked much like they did in the drawing his great-great-grandmother had made long ago that hung on Gray's dining room wall. Many of the families in town had been there nearly as long as his. Gray had always figured that was a good thing.

There was something comforting about the steadfastness of the creeping ivy and old brick walls, the meandering cobblestone streets, and the way the river that circled the outskirts of town trotted along politely between its grassy banks all the way to the Atlantic without ever daring to overflow – except once during a torrential spring downpour when he was twelve. Gray shuddered at the vague faded memory of panicked townspeople and general chaos in the middle of the night. He hoped nothing like that would ever happen again.

And it won't. Not if I have anything to do with it.

Everyone in Baxter Hollow knew each other, knew everything *about* each other, and they always had. It was just a fact of life around there. The same way it was a fact that the cherry trees bloomed in April, the county fair was always held in June, and the town square was neat and well kept – mostly with Gray's own money.

Things were the way they were, and he didn't see any problem with that. Too many places changed just for the sake of changing, brought in big-box stores, fast food, and chain hotels, and look where that got them. *They* certainly weren't the prettiest, most orderly town in New England.

People thought he was funny for being the way he was, young guy and all, so stuffy and stuck in his ways. But Gray liked tradition, he liked comfort and family and familiar surroundings. There wasn't anything wrong with that, he always said. Even if his friends mocked him for it from time to time. Or always.

Gray rarely drove, except to leave town. Nearly everything was reachable on foot – or on bike if he had to do any carrying. Baxter Hollow had stayed small and compact over the years. It never gave into strip-mall sprawl or the mazes of cookie-cutter houses. So, it was a bright September morning that found him walking toward his family's offices carrying Earl Grey tea with milk in the Batman thermos he'd had since second grade, a heated-up breakfast sandwich, and a rather complacent smile.

"Morning, Gray!"

Gray looked up to see his oldest friend, Leo, teetering on the top of a ladder in the middle of repairing Mrs. Brown, the piano teacher's, gutter. He and Leo had known each other their whole lives, since Leo was born to the caretakers of a small apple orchard and cider press that was part of Gray's family estate. Gray and Leo had known Mrs. Brown's sons for years too, although both of them were long since gone, leaving Baxter Hollow for bigger and brighter things.

"Hullo, Leo." Gray nodded and smiled but didn't dare stop to chat.

Leo had a habit of toppling down from tall places when he was distracted. Gray didn't particularly feel like a drive down the highway to the county emergency room. It had happened before, and everyone involved had learned their lesson – don't distract Leo when he's at work.

Leo was a happy guy, easily pleased and content with his place in town. He was always ready with a wave or a smile. Gray's family had offered to fund his tuition to the college of his choice back when Gray had been accepted to Columbia in New York. Leo had opted to stay home in Baxter Hollow and start his own business instead of going to school. Gray often wondered if that hadn't been the better course of action. There hadn't been much in New York for Gray; he didn't like the lights and the noise and the traffic and how everything was so impersonal. He'd been home from Columbia for nearly four years. He didn't plan on leaving again anytime soon.

"See you at the pub for dinner?" Leo called.

"Of course," Gray said back. He scrunched his eyebrows. *Why would today be any different?*

They always met at their friend Sawyer's pub for dinner after work on weeknights – it was far better than any half-assed attempt at cooking he or Leo could make. Leo waved, and his ladder wobbled. He might have fallen to the ground if he hadn't gotten a good hold on Mrs. Brown's downspout. Gray's heart tripped in his chest for a moment before he saw that everything, and everyone was righted.

Gray always walked down Maine Street – he always thought his forefathers had a bit of a sense of humor adding the *e* – and through the town square on his way to the office. His family's building was located kitty-corner to the statue of Benjamin Jonathan Baxter, who'd founded Baxter Hollow back in the early 1700s. He usually stopped to say hello to the man, who was his distant ancestor ... somehow.

Despite his love of Baxter Hollow and the traditions of the area, Gray had never quite grasped the complexities of the family's genealogy; a fact that his mother was rather disappointed with. Madeline Baxter was disappointed with Gray quite a lot. Madeline *Haley*, he reminded himself. His mother was on her second marriage. Jason was a nice enough fellow, Gray supposed, but he wasn't from Baxter Hollow, and they'd been married while Gray was away at college. Gray barely saw him more than once or twice a month, so he hadn't exactly gotten the chance to get close in the past few years.

Which was fine for everyone involved.

When Gray turned the corner into the town square, he inhaled, hoping for another fresh breath of autumn air, leaves and grass and fading sunshine. Instead, he smelled... *tea*? Gray took another long, quizzical sniff. He brought his thermos up to his nose, but no, it was closed tightly, and instead of coming from a certain distinct spot, the scent seemed to be *everywhere*, floating faintly on the breeze. The entire town square smelled like a good cup of brisk Earl Grey, brewed and lightly milked to perfection... and cinnamon toast, just a faint hint, freshly cut grass and vanilla frosting and a wet spring rain. Gray closed his eyes for a moment. *How?* The scent made the hairs on the back of his neck stand. An odd light twisty feeling worked its way through his belly. He wanted to breathe it in and never stop.

Gray opened his eyes once more and looked around as he tried to get the source of that enticing smell that changed on the breeze and made him want to close his eyes and inhale some more. But no – the town square looked just like it always did.

"You all right, man?" Gray turned at the sound of a voice he'd not been expecting. Jake Suarez.

Jake's quiet little bookshop was across the square from Gray's office. He'd been a few years ahead of Gray in school. Mostly, he was a solitary type. Sat in his shop or on the bench outside cozied up in a big wool cardigan, lived with his grand-mother, sold dusty books to tourists driving through town, and smoked expensive cigarettes. Gray didn't really know him, but he knew about him. Just like he knew about everyone.

"I'm fine, thank you." Didn't hurt to be polite. "Do you smell that?"

Jake lifted his cup. That must be it. That was the tea smell. Gray was relieved, ready to write the whole thing off. "I just smell my coffee."

Damn. It wasn't the smell. Gray nodded to hide his growing unease. But just like that, the scent had gone anyway. As soon as he spoke of it aloud, everything went back to normal.

Gray shrugged it off, bid Jake good morning, then wandered across the town square feeling a bit out of sorts. He kept sniffing the air, searching for hints of that tanta-lizing smell. It was really and truly gone.

Maybe I need to get more sleep. That's probably it.

There was an explanation for everything, Gray found. Sleep, or lack thereof, was quite often at the bottom of most things. Gray was all the way in his office before he realized he'd forgotten to say good morning to Benjamin Baxter. He uncapped his thermos and took a long drink of his tea – the normal kind with no elusive hints of vanilla, buttercream or cut grass. Perhaps a bit of caffeine would right his head.

After a restorative gulp of tea, he felt much better. He took out the paperwork he had on his schedule to handle that day. It was a lot of work, managing his family's holdings. But their last property manager had been absolutely useless, and a lot of the properties had fallen into disrepair, rents weren't kept up and taxes were sloppily calculated. Nearly three years later, he was still cleaning up the various messes Mr. Weston Croft had moved all the way from Boston to make. Gray sighed and clicked his pen.

If you want something done the right way…

GRAY HAD FORGOTTEN his lunch at home that morning, which was annoying, to say the least. He'd packed himself soup and a cucumber and salami sandwich from the market, and he'd been looking forward to it for hours. It was a long time until dinner if he contemplated waiting until he got to the pub that evening to eat. Gray looked at his phone. He figured he had time to walk home and get his lunch if he ate the sandwich on the way back to the office. It was a gorgeous day for a change. No rain. Southeastern Maine had been hit with an incredibly wet summer. Of course, now that it was nearly over, it had turned dry, crisp, and pleasant.

He put on his sunglasses and started out across the town square but didn't get far before he saw a bright tow-haired head careening toward him.

"Gray!" She ran into him and wrapped her little arms tight around his waist. His youngest sister – well she'd been the youngest until the new baby, who Gray sometimes forgot about to be honest, came along – had on dark jeans and bright pink Hunter boots. She topped it off with a hot pink Henley that was covered with embroidered sequin hearts. Typical. Gray smiled.

"Hi sweetheart, how are you?"

"Gray, you *have* to talk to Mother," Luna said. "She wants me to go away to school. Like the little lady I am," she finished in a high, prissy voice, clearly mocking how their mother sounded when she wanted to make a point.

It looked like Miss Luna was going to take after him. Gray and his mother had never quite seen eye to eye. He was grateful that other than quarterly reports and a few meetings, she stayed out of his business handling the property management and kept to her own activities.

"Don't you want to go away to school, darling? Have an adventure?" Unless he ran into them in town, Gray rarely saw his sisters for more than the odd visit, even though their family's estate, Baxter House, was only a few minutes' drive out of town. Gray didn't know what his place was in his mother's new marriage, and it was easier to stay where he was in the family townhouse than find out the hard way that he simply didn't belong in their everyday lives anymore.

"No!" Luna cried. "I want to stay here. Can I live with you?"

Gray choked at the idea of his preteen sibling running around his orderly townhouse with lids off her glittery gel pens and sticky treats all over her hands, tearing up the neat back patio with her games. It didn't matter. His mother would never go for it anyway.

"You know you should be with Mom and the girls at home."

"And the new baby," Luna grumbled. "I don't like the new baby. She sleeps all the time and then she *cries*."

Fair enough. Gray hadn't gotten very attached to the

baby either. It felt weird to call the little thing his sister even though they shared the same mother. His thought was interrupted by a loud screech.

"Luna! Mom's going to murder me if you disappear and I don't get you home in time for lunch!" The oldest of Gray's younger sisters, McKenna, came flying across the square much like Luna had – hair askew, handbag and summer jacket barely held on her shoulder. "Oh. Hey, Big G."

Her cheeks were pink, and she was grinning. She looked gorgeous and well taken care of, but a bit dangerous as usual. Gray was wary.

"Mack, slow down," he muttered. He was well aware that the rest of the town watched them. The Baxters, who lived in the big crumbling manor, were the celebrities of the town. "You need to act like the well-bred young lady you are when you're out in public. No shouting. And don't call me Big G."

"Pfft." McKenna rolled her eyes.

She and their middle sister, Fallon, were not like Gray at all. Fallon was busy painting her nails black and listening to music that made Gray's ears melt. McKenna had been dying to escape Baxter Hollow for as long as Gray could remember. She wanted to go to the city and be part of the fast-living New York fashion crowd. She still had a year until she was old enough to go to college. He figured they wouldn't see much of her after that.

"Everyone can suck it," she added.

"*McKenna*. Language. Where's Mom?"

She shrugged. "At home. With the baby." Unlike Luna, McKenna got a dreamy look in her eye at the thought of their little half-sister. That look was quite worrisome to

Gray. He decided to have a chat with their mother quite soon about McKenna's latent interests.

"What are you doing in town?"

"Haven't you heard?" McKenna asked. "Carrie called Mrs. Healey who called Jessica Wilson who called Mom. Somebody's rented out the Pecks' empty café. There's a new guy in town."

Gray felt an odd shiver slink down his back. He thought of that smell from the square that morning and how his whole insides felt all scrambled and floaty afterwards. "New?" he squeaked.

"Yeah. You wanna come check him out with us?"

"*Him?*"

"Yes, Gray. I said new guy." McKenna looked her usual brand of impatient. "That usually implies it's a him."

As soon as his sister said that, it was back. The smell — tea and buttered toast and vanilla and rain, and *yes* it was exactly the same, ephemeral, floating so close, but then it disappeared. Again. And left him with an uncomfortable twist in his gut.

What the hell?

"No. That won't be necessary. I'm pretty busy today. I need to get my lunch and get back to work."

"You know, you don't have to literally take care of all the property just because it's yours." McKenna rolled her eyes. He'd heard her very pointed opinions about his work schedule and self-inflicted sense of responsibility more than once.

"If I don't do it right, who will?" Gray asked.

It was the same thing he'd been asking since their father died all those years ago and left him with *everything*, archaic as that was. Their mother had disappeared into her social calendar, and he was left with three little girls and a lot more than a teenager should handle, even with hired help. But he'd done it then and he still did. Who was going to watch over the girls if Gray didn't? Who was going to watch Baxter House and the other properties and make sure everything was running as it should? Gray had figured out the answer a long time ago. Nobody.

"Come see the new guy with us. You work too hard, G. I mean..."

He listened to his sister, but he wasn't really paying attention. In his mind, all he heard was *new* and *guy*.

He didn't like that weird feeling he'd gotten earlier. Or again just moments before. It wasn't... normal. It wasn't the way Gray liked things to be. Gray wasn't a huge believer in signs, all that kind of stuff was way too woo-woo for him, but he had to agree that if there were things such as signs, that odd flutter in his belly must be one. The way he kept smelling stuff that wasn't there definitely was another. In his life of being perpetually sure of most things, there was one thing that was a simple and clear truth to Gray.

The stranger had to go.